"I'm a big girl, Joel.

"I can tell a guy no if I'm not interested. And I can say yes when I am without needing any brotherly advice."

"Brotherly? You think I'm being brotherly?"

"It isn't necessary, Joel. I'm perfectly capable of—"

"Of knowing when a man wants more from you than friendship?"

"Well, yeah."

"Then it shouldn't surprise you if I do this."

He was wrong, Nic thought as his mouth covered hers. She was more than surprised. She was flabbergasted.

Dear Reader,

My life has been blessed with a happy marriage, three wonderful children and the career I wanted since childhood, but there have been times when the stories inside my head had to compete with more pressing demands. I had just started writing *The Date Next Door* when a tornado hit my home, tearing the roof off my office and doing quite a bit of damage to the rest of the house. While we were grateful that no one was injured and that few of our most treasured possessions were destroyed, the resulting chaos made the writing of this book a daunting prospect. During the long months following the tornado, the book somehow took shape.

As I write this note, I'm only a couple of weeks away from being back in my newly remodeled office. It feels good to know that even when "things" are taken away, the stories are still there waiting to be told. I'm currently concentratating on the next romance taking place in my head, I hope you enjoy meeting Nic Sawyer and Joel Brannon in *The Date Next Door.*

Gina Wilkins

THE DATE NEXT DOOR
GINA WILKINS

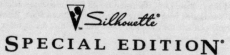

SPECIAL EDITION®

Published by Silhouette Books

America's Publisher of Contemporary Romance

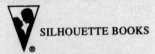

SILHOUETTE BOOKS

ISBN-13: 978-0-373-24799-8
ISBN-10:   0-373-24799-0

THE DATE NEXT DOOR

Visit Silhouette Books at www.eHarlequin.com

Printed in U.S.A.

GINA WILKINS

is a bestselling and award-winning author who has written more than seventy novels for Harlequin and Silhouette Books. She credits her successful career in romance to her long, happy marriage and her three "extraordinary" children.

A lifelong resident of central Arkansas, Ms. Wilkins sold her first book to Harlequin Books in 1987 and has been writing full-time since. She has appeared on the Waldenbooks, B. Dalton and *USA TODAY* bestseller lists. She is a three-time recipient of a Maggie Award for Excellence, sponsored by Georgia Romance Writers, and has won several awards from reviewers of *Romantic Times BOOKreviews*.

For my editor, Patience Smith, who definitely
lived up to her name for this book!

Chapter One

Nicole Sawyer didn't have to be psychic to know it wasn't good when Brad began the conversation with, "We have to talk." Painful experience let her predict his next words. "This isn't about you—it's me."

At twenty-seven, Nic had been down this road enough to know when she was being dumped.

A few awkward but stiffly cordial minutes later, she stood on the porch of her neat frame home and watched Brad's flashy red pickup disappear down the street of her quiet neighborhood. She was going to miss that truck, she thought wistfully. Its seats were comfortable, and the sound system was truly excellent. She had enjoyed riding around town in it, listening to the country music and classic rock they had both favored.

As for the driver…unfortunately their mutual tastes in music hadn't been enough to keep them together. They'd been trying for almost eight months, on and off, to make it work. Brad had finally admitted defeat the day after she had canceled yet another date for work reasons.

She didn't really need him, he had accused her regretfully. And it turned out that he needed to be needed.

Because she knew he was right, she hadn't bothered to argue with him. Though he had tried to be tactful, he hadn't been entirely accurate when he'd said it wasn't her but him. It was always about her, she thought in resignation.

A car door slammed in the driveway next door, and she glanced that way. Her neighbor, Dr. Joel Brannon, stood beside his practical, ecologically friendly little sedan, studying her curiously. He must be planning to go back out that evening, she thought, or he would have parked in his garage.

She wondered fleetingly if he had a date, and if so, with whom. Not that it was any of her business, of course.

"Nic? Everything okay?" he called out.

Joel couldn't have been more opposite from the long, lean, black-haired cowboy who had just driven away. Not particularly tall, he stood perhaps five feet ten, and his build was more sturdy than lanky. His hair was a shade somewhere between light and medium brown, and he kept it cut short because it tended to curl when it grew out. His eyes were hazel and his nose just a little snubbed, but he had a strong chin and a very nice mouth bracketed by shallow dimples.

Nic had once commented to her best friend, Aislinn Flaherty, that Joel reminded her a little of Matt Damon. Aislinn hadn't seen the resemblance.

Because he was still waiting patiently for an answer, she prodded herself to smile and reply, "I'm fine, Joel. Thanks for asking."

Glancing in the direction in which the red truck had disappeared, he asked, "How's Cowboy Brad?"

"Cowboy Brad," she replied prosaically, "is history."

He winced. "I'm sorry. Are you sure you're all right? Do you want to talk?"

Drawing a deep breath, she shook her head, feeling her loose dark blond ponytail brush her neck with the movement. "Thanks, but I'm on duty tonight. I think I'd rather just take a few minutes to myself before I have to change and head into work."

"Sure. But if you need anything at all, you know where to find me."

She nodded and turned toward her door, aware that Joel had meant the offer sincerely. He had become a true friend during the six months or so since he had moved next door to the house where she'd grown up.

It had always been easy for her to have male friends. It was trying to turn those friendships into anything more that seemed to be beyond her capabilities.

* * *

Joel straightened the knot on his tie and studied the result in his bedroom mirror. He was making a speech that evening to a civic group that met once a month at the Western Sizzlin' Restaurant. A jacket and tie seemed to be the required uniform, though he preferred polo shirts and khakis.

Shrugging into his jacket, he looked at the silver-framed photograph on his dresser. "You always did like red ties," he said aloud to the smiling young woman in the picture.

He didn't feel foolish talking to a photo. He'd been doing it for so long it was simply habit now.

Turning away from the dresser, he headed for the doorway, glancing out the bedroom window on his way past. The lights were on next door, but Nic had probably left for work already. She usually left a few lights burning when she worked nights, both for security purposes and because she didn't like returning home to a dark house.

It was a shame about her breakup with the man Joel had nicknamed Cowboy Brad, though he couldn't honestly say it was a surprise. He had been predicting this outcome almost since the day he'd met his neighbor's on-again, off-again boyfriend.

Brad was a decent guy with the type of dark good looks and lazy smiles that seemed to appeal to most women, but he and Nic couldn't have been more mismatched. Though obviously attracted to her fresh-scrubbed sweetness and vibrant personality, Brad had been visibly frustrated with Nic's stubborn independence and deeply ingrained self-sufficiency. He probably wouldn't admit it, but Brad was a very traditional man who would be happiest with a woman who saw him as a protector and a hero.

Officer Nicole Sawyer wasn't that woman.

Wandering into his living room, Joel picked up a small stack of note cards from the coffee table and slipped them into his inside jacket pocket. There was no need to go over his speech; it was a standard spiel about raising safe and healthy children. He had given it a dozen times before. A glance at his watch told him he still had about ten minutes before he needed to leave. Not long enough to do anything much except pace to kill time.

He found his thoughts turning to Nic again. He wondered how she felt about the breakup. As well as Joel thought he understood Brad, he couldn't quite say the same about Nic.

He liked her very much. She was bright, amusing, generous—almost the ideal neighbor. They had often sat on her front porch or his own, taking breaks from yard work and sipping iced tea, chatting with the ease of longtime acquaintances.

Yet those casual conversations had rarely turned personal. They'd shared general information about their families and childhoods but hadn't delved into old wounds. They talked mostly about local gossip and politics, about their jobs as a pediatrician and a police officer, about sports or television programs they both watched.

He knew she lived in the house where she'd grown

up. And that she'd lived there alone since her widowed mother moved to Europe eighteen months earlier to live with Nic's older brother, who worked in an American embassy. Nic knew Joel had grown up in North Carolina and Alabama and had moved to Arkansas after a medical school classmate offered him a partnership in a fledgling pediatrics clinic.

He had told her he'd chosen to buy the house next door to her while driving around aimlessly looking for a neighborhood that felt "right" to him. She hadn't teased him about his method of home shopping; it seemed to have made sense to her when he said that he'd seen the For Sale sign in the yard of this house and had made an offer the next morning.

Nor had she asked, as quite a few others had, why he wasn't interested in living in a more upscale, moneyed area—say, on a golf course or in a gated lakeside lot. Nic seemed to understand that he'd been looking for a private retreat, not a showplace—and for now, that was here.

Joel still couldn't say whether Nic had been in love with her cowboy or had just considered him a pleasant diversion from the demands of her job. He suspected the latter, but since she wasn't one to share her deepest feelings, he couldn't say for sure.

He hoped she hadn't been badly hurt. Nic was too nice a person to have her heart broken. His doctoring skills didn't extend to repairing that particularly painful condition.

He hadn't even been able to fix his own.

* * *

"And then he had the nerve to offer me twenty dollars to tell him who's going to win the football game Monday night. Twenty dollars!"

With indulgent amusement, Nic watched her friend Aislinn Flaherty furiously pace the living room. Aislinn's near-black hair was escaping its neat up-twist, so that long, wispy curls bounced around her indignant face. The midcalf-length tiered brown skirt she wore with a belted camel-colored tunic top whipped around her shapely legs with each forceful turn.

Aislinn made a habit of dressing conservatively almost to the point of blandness, but her efforts were pretty much wasted. She was still striking enough to draw more attention to herself than she would have liked.

"What did you say to that offer?" Nic asked—as if she didn't already know.

"I told him that if I were psychic—which, of course, I am not—I would hardly sell my services so cheaply. And then I told him that if I *had* been psychic, I'd have known better than to agree to a blind date with him."

"So what you're saying is that your date didn't go very well," Nic drawled, smothering a grin.

Aislinn shot her a look of reproval. "This isn't funny, Nic. It was a miserable evening."

Relenting, Nic shook her head. "Sorry. I didn't mean to make light of it. But you have to admit both of us have had some pretty disastrous dates lately."

Actually, Nic had only been out twice since her

breakup with Brad in July, three months ago. Neither outing had been successful enough for a second date with either guy. Since available singles were pretty hard to find in a town the size of Cabot, Arkansas, her social life wasn't looking too promising for the foreseeable future.

"Tell me about it." Plopping onto Nic's brown leather sofa, Aislinn crossed her arms over her shapely chest and pouted. "I should have known better than to let Pamela set me up. She thinks it's so funny to tell everyone I'm…well, different. But I thought I had convinced her to quit saying that."

"You know Pamela. She thinks it's cool to claim to know an honest-to-goodness psychic."

Aislinn sighed gustily. She had been trying for almost all her twenty-eight years to convince everyone that she had no supernatural abilities. She just had "feelings" sometimes, she always added earnestly. Feelings that had an uncanny record of coming true. Nothing more than somewhat-better-than-average intuition, she said.

Having known Aislinn since kindergarten, Nic thought the truth lay somewhere in the middle. She couldn't explain it any better than Aislinn—but she had learned to take her friend's "feelings" seriously.

Aislinn shook her head impatiently. "Enough about my lousy date. How are things going with you?"

Nic unbuckled her heavy utility belt and wearily set her weapon aside. She had gotten home less than twenty minutes earlier, arriving just in time to greet

Aislinn, who had been invited for an evening of pizza and gossip. "Long day."

"The Castleberry break-in?" Aislinn asked sympathetically.

"Yeah. We found evidence that it was Mr. Castleberry's nephew who ransacked the place. Kid's an addict with a record of B and E, but Castleberry couldn't believe the boy would rob the only relative who has stood up for him during the past few years. I think I finally convinced him that there's no room for love or loyalty when drugs take over someone's life."

"I had a feeling it was a male relative. I guess I watch too many of those TV crime shows, despite you making fun of me for it."

"Yeah. Probably." Stretching, Nic rose from the chair she had fallen into to listen to Aislinn's account of last night's unsuccessful date. "Why don't you order the pizza while I change out of my uniform? Help yourself to something to drink—I've got sodas and wine in the fridge."

It was one of the many benefits of being friends for so long, she thought as she emerged from a ten-minute shower and climbed into a pair of purple plaid cotton drawstring pants and a lavender baby T-shirt. She didn't have to stand on formality with Aislinn or bother to entertain her every moment. Leaving her collar-length naturally blond-and-brown hair to dry in a tousled bob, she slid her feet into purple slippers and wandered into the kitchen to rejoin her friend.

Aislinn sat at the kitchen table with a glass of

white wine and the morning newspaper, which Nic hadn't yet had a chance to open. It didn't surprise her that Aislinn had bypassed the headlines and was reading the comic strips instead. Aislinn tended to shy away from crime reports. She never said why, exactly, but Nic suspected it was because Aislinn got too many unsettling "feelings" when she read those grim accounts.

"So did you finish that monster cake today?" she asked, opening the refrigerator to take out a diet soda for herself. "The funky blue one?"

"It isn't blue. It's aquamarine."

"Whatever." Nic carried her soda to the table and helped herself to the sports pages as she took a chair across from Aislinn. "It looked blue to me."

"Trust me. The bride would be very upset if the cake she ordered to exactly match her bridesmaids' hideous aquamarine dresses came out too blue. It matches exactly. And, yes, I finished it."

"How many hours did you put into that one?"

"More than I want to count," Aislinn replied with a groan. "I never again want to see another aquamarine frosting rose."

"The cake really should have been horribly ugly," Nic commented as she glanced over the football scores. "But somehow you made it look really nice—at least, from what I could tell when I saw it yesterday."

Visibly pleased, Aislinn smiled. "Thanks, Nic."

The doorbell rang, and Nic pushed away from the table. "That'll be the pizza. I'll get it."

Glancing over the recipes in the food section of the newspaper, Aislinn nodded absently.

Five minutes later, Nic entered the kitchen again, eying her friend quizzically. "Were you especially hungry when you ordered? Since when have we eaten two pizzas in one night? And why is the second one pepperoni? We always get mushroom and black olive or extra cheese."

Aislinn folded the paper and shrugged. "I just thought we might need extra tonight. If there are any leftovers, we'll divvy them up for cold pizza breakfasts tomorrow morning."

"Sounds good to me." Nic figured it was a good thing she liked cold pizza for breakfast, since it was a safe bet there would be leftovers. Pepperoni wasn't her favorite—or Aislinn's, either, for that matter—but it was food, which pretty well fit her criteria for a meal. She'd never been a picky eater.

She had just set two plates on the table when someone tapped on the back door. She knew that tap. A smile spreading on her face, she moved to respond.

As she had guessed, Joel Brannon stood on her doorstep, his own smile a bit weary but as infectious as ever. There were slight shadows beneath his clear hazel eyes, evidence that he'd been working long hours lately—not that there was anything unusual about that.

"Hi, Joel."

"Hey, Nic," he responded in his pleasant, deep Southern drawl. "I brought back your car vacuum.

Thanks for letting me borrow it. I'm buying one to replace my dead one this weekend."

Accepting the small appliance from him, she nodded. "You're welcome."

He glanced past her and noticed her friend still sitting at the kitchen table. "Oh. Hi, Aislinn. It's nice to see you again."

"Hi, Joel. Have you eaten? Nic and I were just about to have some pizza and we have more than enough if you want to join us."

Though he looked tempted, Joel said, "I wouldn't want to intrude."

"We really do have too much just for the two of us," Nic assured him with only a glance at Aislinn. "You would be doing us a favor to eat some of this pizza."

"Well, since you put it that way..." He closed the door behind him and sniffed the air appreciatively. "Hmm. Smells like pepperoni. My favorite."

Nic didn't even bother to look at Aislinn that time. She simply reached into the cabinet for another plate.

After a ten-hour day at work, it felt good to relax with warm pizza, cold wine and a couple of attractive women—even if one of them made him nervous and the other frequently made him crazy.

Joel glanced at Aislinn Flaherty—the one who made him nervous. And it wasn't just because she was drop-dead gorgeous with her glossy black hair, flawless fair skin, rich chocolate eyes and curvy figure that her bland layered clothing couldn't conceal.

He hadn't spent much time with her, knowing her

only because she was a fairly frequent visitor to his next-door neighbor, but there was something different about Aislinn. He couldn't explain it, exactly. He actually liked her—but sometimes when she looked at him, he had the unsettling sensation that she could see right through him. Much more than he was comfortable revealing.

Nic, on the other hand, was so different from Aislinn that it amazed him sometimes that they were such good friends. There was nothing in the least fey about practical, down-to-earth Nicole Sawyer. Blunt and impatient, Nic was a good cop, a great neighbor and a loyal friend—but not someone he would want as an enemy.

Aislinn interrupted his thoughts with a friendly smile. "Nic and I have been doing all the talking this evening, Joel. I'm afraid we haven't given you much of an opportunity to say anything."

"I've been too busy eating," he replied, indicating his nearly empty plate. "I missed lunch today and I was starving."

"Then it's a good thing we ordered so much, isn't it?" Nic commented, glancing at Aislinn as she spoke.

Aislinn shrugged, but she didn't look away from Joel. "Was it a rough day for you?"

"More long than rough. There's a virus running through several of the local day-care centers, so my waiting room was full of cranky, dehydrated kids."

Nic shook her head. "You've just described my worst nightmare. I'd almost rather face an armed crack addict than a room full of sick, whiny toddlers and their hysterical mothers."

"The toddlers were whiny," he conceded, "but none of the mothers was actually hysterical. And I've got to admit I have absolutely no desire to strap on a gun and face an armed crack addict."

Their respective professions were the basis of a series of running jokes between them. Joel conceded without hesitation that she could probably take him down despite her smaller size.

He was as easygoing as she was intense, as mild-mannered as she was fiery-tempered. He wasn't really intimidated by her, since he knew the kind heart and generous spirit behind her posturing—but he didn't particularly want to make her angry, either.

Aislinn was still looking at him—not rudely but with what appeared to be concern. "Perhaps you're just tired, but there seems to be something bothering you. Is there anything we can do?"

He didn't know how she did it. Maybe, as she insisted, she was simply more intuitive than most people, better able to read facial expressions and body language.

"There's something bugging me a little," he admitted, "but I'll work it out."

The way she studied his face made him wonder if she could actually read his mind. But of course she couldn't, he assured himself a bit too quickly. Her extrasensory talents, if that's what they were, seemed to be more precognitive than telepathic. Not that he believed in stuff like that, of course.

"Nic and I are pretty good at brainstorming," she said. "Why don't you try us?"

"Yeah, Joel," Nic seconded. "Aislinn and I are always dumping problems on each other and usually we come up with some sort of solution. We'd be happy to talk about what's bothering you if you want to discuss it. If not, just tell us to butt out and we'll change the subject."

He had always found it easy to be with Nic. Comfortable. He liked the way she treated him. Like a regular guy. Not an eligible bachelor-doctor. Or worse—a tragically romantic figure. Women usually classified him as one or the other, sometimes an uncomfortable combination. Nic simply saw him as her neighbor and friend.

Maybe she would understand the dilemma that had been weighing on him for the past couple of weeks....

"What happened?" she asked encouragingly. "Is it one of your patients?"

"No, nothing like that. It's—this is going to sound pretty silly," he said with an irritated shake of his head.

"Try us."

He looked into the two inquiring faces turned toward him and sighed.

"My high school class back in Alabama is having an informal fifteen-year reunion in a couple of weeks. They're attending the homecoming football game, which is against a big rival, and then having several activities and a dance the next day, followed by a farewell breakfast on Sunday morning. I'm just dreading it, that's all."

Aislinn's expression didn't change in response to Joel's revelation. Nic looked surprised, but he couldn't blame her for that. He doubted that she had expected a mere high school reunion to be his dilemma. But then, she didn't know the whole story.

"A fifteen-year reunion?" she repeated.

He nodded. "Our class secretary was Heidi Pearl. Heidi Rosenbaum now. If it were up to her, we'd get together every year. Thank goodness the class confines her to having reunions only once every five years."

"Did you go to the last one?"

"Yeah." He figured his tone gave her an indication of how awful that had been.

Nic shrugged. "Last I heard, there's no law that says you have to attend high school reunions. I'm not sure I'll go to my ten-year reunion next summer. I've got better things to do than to sit around with a bunch of people I barely know now, talking about embarrassing adolescent memories. Aislinn's the only friend I held on to from high school, and she and I see each other often enough."

"Yeah, but I'm kind of expected to go. I was the class president."

"Of course you were," Nic murmured.

He gave her a mild look, then added, "Besides, Heidi works for my dad. There aren't any excuses that would hold up to her daily inquisitions."

"She sounds kind of scary."

"Trust me. She's terrifying."

Nic chuckled, then shook her head. "Still. You should just tell them you aren't interested this time."

"I wish I could."

"Why can't you?"

"You wouldn't understand."

"Try me," she said again.

"I think she will understand," Aislinn said, making him wonder if she had somehow already guessed his quandary. Good intuition, he reminded himself. Nothing more.

The funny thing was, he thought maybe Nic *would* understand. One of the few women in the small-town Arkansas police department where she worked, she was well accustomed to trying to meet everyone else's expectations.

"Judging from past experience," he said, trying to choose his words carefully, "if I go, I'll be greeted with cloying sympathy and treated like some kind of tragic hero. If I don't go, everyone will be even more convinced that I'm an emotional basket case."

"You? A basket case?" Nic's eyes were wide with surprise beneath her fringe of blond-streaked bangs. "You're, like, the sanest, most normal guy I know."

"Yes, well, I wasn't in such good shape the last time my class got together, five years ago. My wife, Heather, had died only a few months earlier, and I— Well, I guess I wasn't ready for a reunion of all my old high school friends."

"Heather was in your class?" Aislinn asked, her slightly husky voice warm with compassion.

He nodded. "We were typical high school sweethearts. We went to the prom together, were voted 'cutest couple,' that sort of thing. We attended different universities, but we stayed together despite the odds against long-distance relationships. Then I went to medical school and she to graduate school—again, different schools, different states. We got engaged during Christmas break of our third years but waited until we felt financially ready before we got married."

He took a sip of his soda before adding tonelessly, "Six months later, she was killed in a car accident. Broadsided by a semi with bad brakes."

Chapter Two

Nic had known, of course, that Joel was a young widower. He had mentioned once that his wife died in a car accident, but she hadn't asked for any details, nor had he volunteered any.

He hadn't been in any relationships during the months she had known him, and she had wondered if he was still grieving for the wife he'd lost. Now that she knew how long Joel and Heather had been together, she understood exactly how hard that loss must have been for him.

"I'm sorry," she said, not knowing what else to say.

It seemed to be enough. He nodded. "Anyway, I made the mistake of attending the reunion before I'd completely worked through my grieving, and it was a…rough experience. Too many painful reminders, too much emotion and sympathy from my class-mates. I was a mess by the time it was over and I didn't do a very good job of hiding it."

"That's understandable," she assured him. "It would have been a difficult ordeal for anyone."

He searched her face as if trying to tell whether she really did understand. Apparently satisfied with whatever he saw there, he nodded again. "The thing is, that was five years ago. I've come a long way since then. I've made peace with my past. I've made a good life for myself here and I consider myself a generally happy guy."

"That's the impression I've always had of you." Actually, she considered him the most laid-back and easygoing man she knew. She'd often envied him his ability to take things in stride, handling the pres-sures of his job with apparent ease.

"It's not an act," he assured her. "That's really the way I feel, for the most part."

"That's good then, right? So your old friends should be pleased to see you doing so well."

Joel squirmed a little in his chair. "I'm just not so sure they'll see it that way. I'm afraid they'll still view me as the man I was rather than the one I've become."

"A legitimate concern," Aislinn agreed.

Nic shrugged. "So don't go. Send your best wishes to all your old friends, tell them you're doing great but you're too busy with work to join them this time."

"That would probably be best, of course…"

"But it isn't what you want to do," Aislinn translated from his expression. "Why not?"

Looking rather sheepish, he replied, "I think it's a pride thing."

If there was anything Nic could understand, it was a "pride thing." She had been accused on plenty of occasions of having entirely too much pride for her own good.

Comprehension clicked in her brain. "You don't want your old friends to think you can't handle another reunion. You're afraid if you don't go, they'll think it's because you're still too wounded and vulnerable. That's what you meant by *basket case*."

Wincing a little at her choice of adjectives, he nodded. "I guess that's it. The only way to convince them that I'm really okay seems to be to show up and prove it. But…well, it still won't be easy."

Aislinn seemed to have a sudden brainstorm. "What you should do," she said earnestly, "is take someone with you. You know, like a date or something. That way everyone can see that you're okay, and the attention won't all be focused on you."

"Take someone with me?" The suggestion seemed to startle him. "I hadn't even thought of that."

"What better way to demonstrate that you've moved on?" Nic asked, seeing the logic of Aislinn's idea. She hoped she wasn't coming across as insensitive to Joel's loss—but he was the one who had said he'd put the past behind him. And tact had never been her strong point, unfortunately.

Joel didn't seem to take offense at her wording. Instead he appeared intrigued by her reasoning. "I wouldn't want to make any pretense about a relationship that doesn't exist. No fake romances or anything like that."

Nic exchanged a wince with Aislinn before replying, "Oh, agreed. Ick. Just introduce your companion as a friend and leave it at that. The others can make what they want out of it."

Still looking thoughtful, Joel toyed with a pizza crust on his plate. "It's a good idea, but I wouldn't know who to ask. Unless…is there any way I could talk you into going with me, Nic?"

Nic could almost feel her jaw drop. "You would want *me* to go with you?"

"Well, you would be the logical choice," he replied. "We're friends. We have a good time together. If I asked someone else, I'd have to get into sticky explanations, whereas you already know the whole story. I heard you tell Aislinn earlier that you could use a few days away from work. I know attending someone else's reunion is hardly an ideal vacation, but I'd make sure you have a good time. And I'd owe you big-time."

He had spoken so quickly that she'd had a hard time following him. But it all came down to the realization that he was asking her to accompany him to his high school reunion. The fact that she had concurred with Aislinn's recommended plan didn't make Joel's invitation any less startling. "I, uh—"

Embarrassed now, he lifted one shoulder in a

shrug. "Never mind. Bad idea. I can't blame you for not wanting to have anything to do with this."

"Well, it was our idea," she conceded, motioning toward Aislinn, who was watching them in silence.

"Yeah, but you weren't volunteering to be the attention deflector. I understand."

"Isn't there anyone else you can take?"

"Not really. Like I said, I don't want to go through a bunch of explanations again, nor do I want to give anyone the wrong idea by asking her to my reunion. It wouldn't be fair for me to risk using anyone just for the sake of my own pride."

There was that word again. *Pride.* The one argument she understood best.

Maybe she couldn't really understand Joel's dilemma in its entirety, especially since she had never viewed him as a "tragic figure" herself, but she could understand his need to prove himself to other people. She'd been doing that herself for most of her life.

"Okay," she blurted. "I'll go."

Aislinn murmured her approval of Nic's impulsive acceptance.

Joel blinked. "Um—you'll go?"

She nodded before she could talk herself out of the rash offer. Joel was a friend, she reminded herself, and she didn't have many real friends. Friends came through for each other. "I'll go if you really think it will help you out. But I warn you, I'm lousy at parties and social events. You might very well regret asking me when I embarrass you in front of all your old schoolmates."

His smile made a funny little shiver run down her spine. "Not possible."

It wasn't the first time she had noticed how attractive he was. Not even the first time she'd found herself reacting rather dramatically to that attractiveness. Only natural, of course, with her being a normal single woman and Joel being so darned sexy. But she neither expected—or even wanted—anything to develop between them.

She liked having him as her friend. And from painful experience, she had learned that nothing ruined a great friendship faster than trying to turn it into more.

The mental warnings she had been trying to ignore since she'd accepted his offer began to clang more loudly, harder to discount now. As much as she disliked social events, as much as she dreaded attending a reunion of strangers who would be studying her with curiosity, she was beginning to worry that the greatest peril inherent in this scheme wasn't making a fool of herself or embarrassing Joel.

It made an interesting—and frustrating—dilemma. By doing Joel a big favor in the name of friendship, was she taking the risk of damaging that relationship that had become so special to her during the past few months?

Declining the ice cream Nic offered for dessert, Joel left not long after the discussion about his reunion. Aislinn lingered to help Nic clean up the remains of their dinner.

"It was nice of you to agree to help him," she said when she and Nic were alone.

Nic looked at her friend suspiciously. "Why do I get the feeling that you somehow manipulated me into agreeing?"

"I had nothing to do with it. He needed your help, and you came through—as you always do for people you care about."

Nic closed the dishwasher door with a little slam. "Because I'm a sucker, right?"

"No. Because you have a good heart," Aislinn said loyally. "And because there's very little you wouldn't do for your friends."

"Yeah, well, I might have gone a little too far this time. I don't suppose you knew what he was going to ask me to do?"

"No. I just had a feeling there was something you could do to ease his mind—and I knew you would do it."

"But…a high school reunion, Aislinn. With a bunch of strangers even Joel doesn't seem too enthusiastic about. Can you imagine how awful that's going to be?"

"It would have been worse for him to go alone. We can both understand why he wouldn't want to be treated as an object of pity. And you and Joel are such good friends that he knows you'll probably have a good time despite the awkwardness of the situation."

"I'm sure that's why he thought I'd be the one to take with him. Because we get along well without having to worry about any complicated undercurrents between us," Nic said lightly, wanting to make sure Aislinn wasn't getting any wrong ideas. "And, of course, he's hesitant to take another date because he doesn't want to lead anyone on—apparently that's a problem for a single doctor."

"Especially one who looks like Joel," Aislinn murmured.

A mental image of crowds of hopeful women chasing after Joel made Nic scowl. "I guess that's why he was comfortable asking me. He can be confident that I see him as a pal, nothing more."

"Hmm."

Nic frowned more deeply. "What's that supposed to mean?"

"It didn't mean anything," her friend replied innocently. "I was just responding to you."

Though she was still suspicious of Aislinn's tone—they had been friends for too long to deceive each other easily—Nic decided to just let it go for now. For some reason, she felt as though they were edging a little too close to potentially dangerous territory.

"Maybe you'll have a good time," Aislinn said after the silence had stretched a bit too long.

"And maybe I'll win the lottery and become the country's newest multimillionaire—which would be even more miraculous since this state doesn't have a lottery," Nic shot back. "But I'm going, okay? And Joel is *so* going to owe me after this. Big-time."

"I'm sure he'll be happy to pay up," Aislinn said, now looking just a bit too bland.

Once again Nic decided to let the comment pass without response.

* * *

"You're sure you don't mind doing this?" On the Friday morning of Joel's reunion, he stood with one hand on the open trunk of his car, studying Nic's face. He had just placed her bag inside with his own, but he was giving her one last chance to change her mind about accompanying him to his hometown.

She settled the issue by reaching up to place her hand next to his, pushing down to close the trunk with a decisive snap. "It's too late to change our plans now. I've already arranged to take off work today. I'm not expected back until Monday morning."

"Still, you could do something with your time off that would be more fun than bailing me out of a jam."

"Dude, we've had this conversation a dozen times in the past two weeks. Now get in the car before you talk me into changing my mind."

Chuckling ruefully at her tone, Joel opened the passenger door for her, then walked around to slide behind the wheel. "I really do appreciate this, Nic."

"Look," she said, snapping her seat belt. "let's just agree that you've already thanked me enough, okay? There's no need to keep doing so all weekend."

"Okay. But I am grateful," he added in a mutter.

She sighed heavily, making him chuckle again.

They left his car in the parking deck at the Little Rock Regional Airport and went through the lengthy process of checking in and going through security.

Joel had insisted on buying Nic's ticket, though she had offered to pay her own way.

This trip was on him, he had informed her. It wasn't as if it would have been her first choice of a long-weekend destination.

It wasn't a long flight from Little Rock to Birmingham, Alabama, and the time passed quickly. Too quickly, as far as Nic was concerned. As determined as she was to do everything she could to help Joel out this weekend, she was in no real hurry to get started.

A man with clear hazel eyes exactly like Joel's met them at the airport in Birmingham. As he and Joel greeted each other with warm smiles and hearty slaps on the shoulder, Nic studied Ethan Brannon curiously. Not so much the Matt Damon resemblance here, she decided. Ethan's face was more sharply planed than Joel's, a bit harder, even when he smiled.

He was smiling when he turned to her, taking the hand she offered when Joel introduced her casually as his friend and neighbor. But this smile was different from the one he'd shared with his younger brother, she saw immediately. This was the polite, rather cool smile he might offer a stranger he didn't quite know whether to trust.

Still, his tone was friendly enough when he said, "Nicole, it's a pleasure to meet you. Joel's told me about you. You're the police officer, aren't you?"

"Yes, I am. And please call me Nic. Everyone does."

He nodded and turned back to Joel. "Let's get your bags."

"We've got them." Both Joel and Nic had packed light for the weekend, stuffing everything they needed into wheeled carry-on bags. Joel had teased her about bringing so much less than he'd expect from a woman, but she'd gotten the impression he wasn't particularly surprised. "Let's go."

Nic sat in the backseat of Ethan's SUV, giving the brothers a chance to catch up during the hour-long drive to their parents' house in small-town Danston, Alabama. She watched the interaction between them during the trip, making several private observations.

Ethan was very much the older brother, she decided. A little bossy. A bit too concerned about Joel's well-being, as if it were his responsibility to make sure younger brother was okay.

Nic knew that dynamic all too well, having an older brother of her own. Paul had displayed a tendency to go overboard with advice about her life, too, until she had rebelled at twenty and informed him in no uncertain terms that she didn't need his guidance, even if it meant she had to make a few mistakes along the way.

She wondered if Joel had ever had that talk with Ethan. After all, Joel was thirty-three, long past the stage when Nic had asserted her independence.

Maybe the difference was that Ethan was a bit more subtle about it than Paul had been. He wasn't openly snooping or issuing advice, just asking questions and wondering aloud why Joel had made certain decisions—such as moving to Arkansas when he could have had a thriving practice in Birmingham or Atlanta.

"If you'd wanted a small-town practice, you could have stayed in Danston," he added, letting his voice rise just enough to turn the statement into an implied question.

"I needed to get away from Danston," Joel replied with a shrug, and though his tone was unemotional, his simple words expressed a great deal.

Ethan must have picked up on that implied message. He let the subject drop. "So, Nic," he said, "what bribe did my brother use to talk you into coming to his reunion with him?"

She laughed. "No bribe. Just lots of manipulation. And he does owe me a favor after this."

"No kidding. I still live here in town and *I* don't go to my reunions."

"The difference is that no one expects you to," Joel muttered.

"No. The difference is that I don't particularly care what anyone else expects of me," Ethan returned smoothly.

Joel let that pass.

"We're almost to my parents' house, Nic," Ethan said, looking at her in the rearview mirror. "I'm sure you'll be glad to stretch and freshen up."

"I'll be staying at a motel, won't I?"

"Are you kidding? Mom's got the guest room all ready for you. She's been fussing over it for days."

"Oh, I didn't want her to go to that much trouble." Nic frowned at the back of Joel's head, knowing he had deliberately withheld that bit of information from her. "I told you I would be perfectly comfortable in a motel or at the resort where the rest of your out-of-town classmates are staying."

"Stay by yourself at a motel? Mother would have a fit. She's pretty old-fashioned that way. And we'll be spending enough time at the resort as it is. You wouldn't want to be stuck there with my old friends while I'm visiting with my family. This way we can leave together when things get boring—as I'm sure they will."

Nic twined her fingers more tightly in her lap, regretting—not for the first time—that she had ever let herself get talked into coming along.

Chapter Three

Nic was not a particularly tall woman. Five feet six inches in her sensible work shoes, she was usually several inches shorter than the men she confronted daily on the job. She stayed slim and muscular through a combination of regular exercise and overactive metabolism. Yet still she felt as though she towered over Joel's mother, Elaine Brannon.

Elaine reminded her vividly of the delicate porcelain figurines her grandmother had collected, and which Nic had been sternly forbidden to touch. Elaine might have stood five feet two on her tallest days and was hardly large enough to cast a shadow. Though neither of her sons topped six feet, she was dwarfed between them, her impeccably made-up face glowing with pride as she gazed up at them.

As Ethan's had earlier, Elaine's smile changed when she turned to greet Nic. If a smile could be gracious and suspicious at the same time, this one was.

Nic was almost amused. Apparently this family worried that Joel would be the target of unscrupulous gold diggers or doctor groupies, even though she knew he had told them that she and Joel were just friends. Even if they incorrectly suspected there was more to their relationship, did they honestly think she looked like either of those types? She wore just enough makeup to satisfy her mother. There was no expensive "product" in her casual, easy-to-maintain hairstyle. She couldn't show cleavage if she tried, since she didn't particularly have any.

Joel saw her as a pal, not a potential romantic partner—and that was exactly the way she wanted things to remain. Much less messy all around.

The woman's tiny hand was icy-cold in Nic's. "Welcome to our home, Nicole," Elaine said with practiced Southern charm. "My husband hasn't returned from work yet, but he's looking forward to meeting you."

"Thank you, Mrs. Brannon. It really wasn't necessary for you to put me up, you know. I could have stayed in a motel."

Elaine shook her ash-blond head. "What kind of hosts would we be if we sent you off to a motel? I've prepared the guest room for you and I hope you'll be comfortable in it."

"I'm sure I will be," Nic lied politely, though the privacy of an anonymous motel room sounded very nice at the moment.

"Come on, Nic, I'll show you to your room so you can freshen up," Joel offered, motioning toward the stairway that curved upward behind them.

She followed him gratefully, aware that both his mother and brother were watching as she and Joel climbed the stairs.

The average-size four-bedroom house was fashioned in a vaguely Colonial style with gleaming wood floors, wainscoted walls and reproduction light fixtures. It was warm and welcoming, not too formal for Nic's tastes and yet attractively decorated. Framed family photographs adorned almost every inch of the walls of the upstairs hallway.

She stopped at a large family portrait, recognizing a much younger Elaine immediately. Elaine had aged very well, looking barely different now. A man stood beside her, and it was obvious where Ethan and Joel had gotten their similar features. "Is this your father?"

"Yes. That's Dad—Lou Brannon. He should be home soon. I think you'll like him."

"I'm sure I will." But her attention had turned to the children in the photo.

Ethan and Joel were easy enough to spot; neither of them had changed significantly since toddlerhood, apparently. Yet it was the other child whose image held her riveted, another boy, this one little more than a baby, perhaps a couple of years younger than Joel. "This little boy…"

"My younger brother. Kyle."

Sadness filled her as she realized the significance of his never mentioning Kyle to her before. Studying the happy, innocent face in the photo, she bit her lower lip.

"He died in a flash flood twenty-eight years ago. He was almost two."

Though Joel had spoken without emotion, Nic knew him well enough to understand that his rather flat, even tone was an attempt to hide exactly how strongly he did feel about the loss of his younger brother. "I'm sorry."

"I barely remember him," Joel replied with a slight shrug. "I was just four myself. He was with his nanny when her car was swept into a flooded river. The car was eventually found, but neither the nanny's nor my brother's bodies were inside. They were never recovered."

Nic thought of the woman she had met downstairs, and her gaze turned back to Elaine's face in the portrait. She looked so young, so proud of her attractive family. Nic couldn't imagine what she had gone through when she'd lost her youngest child.

"I'm very sorry," she said again.

He nodded and motioned down the hallway. "The guest room is at the end of the hall—next door to the room where I'll be sleeping."

She couldn't resist pausing to look at several more of the family photographs, amused by the images of Joel as a gap-toothed, towheaded little boy, self-conscious in front of the camera. Oddly enough, Ethan looked almost as somber and responsible as a child as he did now. Had he been born an old soul? The mental question made her smile, as it sounded more like something Aislinn would ponder than herself.

Her amusement faded when she studied the photographs of a more mature Joel. Eagle Scout, high school graduate, college graduate, medical school graduate—all of his accomplishments had been recorded and displayed in this family hall of fame. It was during high school that he began to be accompanied in many of the photos by a strikingly lovely redhead. Tall, curvy, intelligent-looking, the woman seemed to be as at home within those frames as Joel and his brother and parents.

"This is Heather," she murmured.

"Yes." He glanced at a wedding photo of himself and his late bride. "This was taken six months before she died."

It was a good thing, Nic mused, that she didn't have any romantic designs on Joel. It would be hard to compete with the memory of this supermodel-beautiful woman.

The Brannons had certainly known their share of tragedy, yet the general impression she received from this neatly crowded photo gallery was of a close, generally happy clan. Her own family had also suffered loss, she thought with a fleeting memory of her father's last cancer-racked days. And they, too, had been able to put the pain behind them and move on with their lives, though of course it had been difficult for her mother.

That life could be hard and often unfair was something Nic had learned a long time ago. She had decided to concentrate as much as possible on the positives, a philosophy she knew she shared with Joel. So why did his old friends seem determined to focus on his tragedies rather than his accomplishments? Or was that situation mostly in his own imagination?

She supposed she would be finding out soon enough. They would be meeting his old classmates in less than three hours. Swallowing hard, she looked away from the photograph of beautiful Heather Brannon and followed Joel into the guest room.

"Joel told us you're a police officer, Nicole. That must be a challenging career for a petite young woman like yourself."

It was one of the first comments orthodontist Lou Brannon made after being introduced to Nic. She recognized his tone. He was one of those people who was equally fascinated and dismayed by her career choice. His only knowledge of the job probably came from television and crime novels, and he couldn't imagine why anyone, especially a woman, would want to spend every day pursuing criminals and other lowlife.

"I enjoy it," she said, as she always did to such comments. "And it pays my bills."

They were standing in the den, chatting for a few minutes with Lou and Elaine before Joel and Nic had to leave for the pregame gathering of his classmates.

"It's such a dangerous and unsavory job," Elaine

fretted. "I can't imagine why any young woman would want to do it."

An awkward moment of silence followed that comment. Nic finally responded with a simple, "I like it."

"And she does it very well," Joel said in an attempt to smooth over the slight tension his mother's remarks had left between them. "She's received several commendations just in the relatively short time she's been on the force."

Being no more comfortable with Joel's compliments than his mother's criticisms, Nic abruptly changed the subject. "What time are we supposed to leave for the reception?"

He checked his watch. "Pretty soon. We're meeting at Chucky's Bar and Grill at six for drinks before the seven-thirty kickoff. Chucky's is less than a mile from the football field, so everyone's going to caravan over after drinks."

"How many were in your class?"

"Just under a hundred. Not exactly a big school, so we all pretty much knew each other."

Elaine smiled mistily—something which must have taken quite a bit of practice, Nic decided with a dose of cynicism. "Joel and Heather were so popular and outgoing that their classmates all knew them and loved them. Especially Heather. I don't believe she ever said an unkind word about anyone in her entire life."

Nic could hardly make the same claim. She pushed her hands into the pockets of the black twill slacks she wore with a black-and-purple color-block turtleneck sweater and waited silently for Joel to announce that it was time to leave. She was greatly relieved when he did so almost immediately.

"Sorry about my mother," Joel said as he guided his father's borrowed car away from his parents' home. "Sometimes she speaks without really thinking about how it sounds."

"Your mother has been perfectly nice to me," Nic assured him blandly.

He shot a skeptical glance her way. "I saw the way you looked when she talked about your job. You were biting your tongue until it almost bled when she said she couldn't imagine why you'd want to do it."

"Why any 'young woman' would want to do it," Nic corrected him, giving up the pretense that it hadn't bothered her. "Insert *well-bred* in front of *young,* of course, because that's what she really meant."

"Mom's just kind of traditional, that's all. She's modern enough to defend your right to pursue any career you want and your capability to perform the job well—but she's old-fashioned enough to think of being a cop as a man's work. She would probably have reacted the same way if you'd said you were a firefighter."

Gazing out the side window at the small-town scenery passing by, Nic twisted her fingers in her lap. "You said your wife went to graduate school. What did she do?"

"She earned a Ph.D. in psychology. She was a family counselor."

"I suppose your mother approved of that career for a woman."

"You really did take offense, didn't you? I'm sorry, Nic, but I hope you don't believe she meant to insult you."

Nic shook her head and forced a smile. "Forget it. I wasn't really offended. It isn't the first time anyone's suggested I was crazy for wanting to be a cop."

Which was the truth, of course. Her own parents hadn't exactly cheered when she'd announced her intention to enter the police academy. Her overprotective big brother had been even less enthusiastic, worrying aloud that her small size would put her at risk.

She had long since convinced her family that she was doing exactly what she wanted to do—and doing it well. Other people had mocked or criticized her job, and she rarely took offense. So why had it been different with Joel's parents?

"My mom doesn't think you're crazy, okay? She just doesn't know you yet."

And wasn't sure she wanted to, Nic added silently. Elaine had obviously been trying to decide just how far Joel's friendship with Nic went. And she hadn't been at all certain she wanted her son the doctor to be involved with a cop.

It was clear that Nic and Joel were going to have to remind his family, especially his mother, that they were only friends.

Chucky's Bar and Grill might have sounded like

a dark, smoky dive, but the place was well lit, decorated in cheery, bright colors and openly welcoming when Joel escorted Nic inside. Country music played in the background, almost drowned out by the sounds of laughter and conversation, and beer foamed in thick glass mugs being distributed by black-aproned waitresses of assorted ages.

Approximately forty people had gathered for the reunion, mostly in their early thirties, of course. Nic saw at once that this was no highbrow country-club crowd, for the most part, at least. Most of them looked working-class, a few sporting the mullets and tattoos one might expect in a small Southern town. Almost everyone wore red, an observation that made her realize abruptly that Joel wore a bright red long-sleeve polo shirt with khaki slacks.

"Let me guess," she said. "Your team color was red."

"Red and white." He shrugged a bit sheepishly. "I suppose I forgot to mention it. It's just habit for me to stick on a red shirt when I watch the Cardinals play."

"The Danston Cardinals?"

He grinned. "The lifeblood of this town. Danston's social and cultural life revolves around the school—athletics, music, drama, dances. And tonight's game is against our archrival, another small town that feels exactly the same way about their team, the Penderville Pirates."

Nic could certainly understand a heated rivalry. She enjoyed sports and she was a fierce competitor herself on the department softball team. For that matter, she had been known to execute some pretty impressive—and highly illegal—tackles during games of flag football. She might not be looking forward to the rest of this reunion, but she was always in the mood to watch a spirited football game, even between two high school teams.

"Joel! You made it."

The squeal had issued from a woman with blond-highlighted hair sprayed into a stiff, too-cute spiky style. The right colors of makeup had been applied a bit too heavily. Cushiony cleavage spilled out of a scoop-neck red sweater, and ample hips were buttoned into stretchy jeans. Splashy jewelry dangled from her ears and wrists and glittered on red-manicured fingers. Yet the woman's smile was warm and generous as she gazed up at Joel with unmistakable pleasure. "It's so good to see you. You look wonderful."

He bent his head to brush a light kiss against her cheek. "Thanks, Heidi. And you look radiant as always."

Heidi blushed rosily. "You certainly inherited your daddy's charm. Unlike your older brother, I might add."

Joel chuckled. "Ethan was born grumpy. But he's a good guy."

"I didn't say he wasn't. He just doesn't often bother with the little pleasantries." She turned then toward Nic, her round face alight with visible curiosity. "Aren't you going to introduce me to your friend?"

"Of course." Joel reached out to pull Nic a bit closer, resting one hand lightly at the small of her back. "Heidi Rosenbaum, this is my friend from Arkansas, Nicole Sawyer."

Heidi's manicured hand was impossibly soft when she placed it in Nic's unpolished, slightly more callused hand. "It's nice to meet you, Nicole. You're from Arkansas? So I assume you didn't attend Penderville High."

A bit confused, Nic shook her head. "I went to school in Cabot, where I still live, next door to Joel. Why?"

Heidi motioned toward Nic's sweater. "Purple and black are the colors of the Penderville Pirates. The team we're playing tonight."

Suppressing a groan, Nic managed a wry smile. "I didn't know. But I promise I'll cheer like crazy for the Cardinals."

Heidi giggled. "Good. They're going to need all the support they can get."

"Heidi!" someone called from another part of the room. "Come tell Jessica who was Student Council secretary our senior year. I think it was Janet, but she thinks it was Kelly."

Heidi rolled her eyes. "Of course it was Kelly," she called back. "And if she wasn't having a baby in Birmingham even as we speak, she would take a piece out of your hide for forgetting that."

Turning back to Nic, she confided, "Kelly was very proud of being elected that year. She'd run and lost three times before."

"Oh." Exactly what was Nic expected to say in response to that tidbit?

"Anyway, you wouldn't be interested in that. Would you like a glass of wine? The house white isn't too bad here."

"Actually, I'd rather have a beer," Nic replied, eying a tray full of invitingly frosty mugs.

"Oh." Heidi blinked once or twice, as if surprised by Nic's answer, but then she smiled at Joel. "Your friend knows what she likes, doesn't she?"

Nic's left eyebrow rose quizzically. Just what was *that* supposed to mean?

Another shout came from the group sharing memories on the other side of the room. "Heidi—who was historian?"

With a dramatic groan and a shake of her head, Heidi murmured an excuse to Joel and Nic and left to join her other old friends.

"Heidi knows everything there is to know about this class. Past, present—and probably future," Joel murmured into Nic's ear.

"You know what I said about her sounding a little scary when you told me about her? Turns out I was right."

Joel laughed and nudged her toward the bar. "Let's get you that beer. Then I'll introduce you to some *really* scary people."

Nic couldn't remember ever wanting a drink more.

Chapter Four

Nic could almost feel the eyes trained on them as she and Joel crossed the room to the bar, Joel returning greetings along the way. There was open curiosity in those eyes, combined with speculation about her role in Joel's life. She knew she looked much different than the stunning redhead they remembered with him. And while she rarely fretted about her appearance, taking for granted that she looked okay, she was well aware that she wasn't the beauty Heather had been.

Not that it mattered, of course. She'd resigned herself years ago to descriptions like "cute" and "pleasant." She'd even learned to be satisfied with that image, though cuteness wasn't exactly an advantage in her job. And since she wasn't competing with the memory of a tall, gorgeous redhead for Joel's romantic interest, there was no reason for her to mind the comparisons.

Two beefy, eerily identical men with shaved heads and goofy smiles approached them a few minutes later, simultaneously slapping Joel on the back hard enough to slosh the beer in his just-filled mug. "Joel Brannon," they bellowed in perfect unison. "It's good to see you, man."

Somehow, through some process Nic couldn't imagine, Joel correctly identified each twin as he greeted them. "Hey, Ernie. Hey, Earl. How've you both been?"

Ernie answered, "We're doing great. Me and Kay have three kids now. Earl and Cassie have two. Hellions, the lot of 'em."

Laughing at the affectionate summary, Joel introduced Nic. The Watson twins greeted her much the way Heidi had—warmly but with open curiosity about her relationship to their old friend.

Introductions out of the way, Joel asked, "Are you guys still working in your dad's heat-and-air business?"

"Running it now," Earl corrected. "Dad retired last year."

"Yeah? How's he doing?"

"He's loving the leisurely life," Ernie said. "Fishing, hunting, playing dominoes over at the VFW. Driving Mom crazy."

Joel laughed. "Good for him."

"Hey, you remember the Penderville game our

senior year? When you threw that sixty-yard pass to Gonzalez?"

Groaning, Joel took a sip of his beer before answering, "We lost—35 to 14."

"Yeah, but that was one hell of a pass."

"Sure impressed the cheerleaders," Ernie said with a waggle of his heavy eyebrows. "'Specially the captain of the squad."

Earl cleared his throat and punched his brother in the ribs. He might have tried to be subtle about it, but he couldn't have been more obvious—and Ernie got the message. His round face reddening, he muttered, "Uh, sorry, Joel."

Joel's expression didn't change. "No problem. As I remember, impressing the captain of the cheerleading squad was my top priority that year. Might have explained why I was such a mediocre athlete."

The brothers responded with weak smiles and a quick, awkward change of subject. It was no stretch for Nic to figure out who the captain of the cheerleading squad had been.

Heather's shadow hovered behind them through the rest of the reception as Joel worked the room, casually introducing Nic as his friend from Arkansas, ignoring the questions in his old schoolmates' faces. It was so obvious that everyone was carefully avoiding any mention of Joel's late wife, which made it all the more apparent that they were thinking of her. Quite naturally, of course, since she had been a prominent member of their class.

Saying little, Nic watched them interact with Joel.

There was no doubt that he was well liked and respected. Several of the other guests cornered him with medical questions, both about themselves and their children, but he handled it with practiced ease. He had a little more trouble handling their sympathy, which was always implied and sometimes almost blatant in soulful looks or syrupy tones.

She could see now what he had meant when he'd said he was tired of being treated like a saint or a pity case. Everyone was simply trying too hard to keep from reminding him of his loss. They even seemed almost apologetic about mentioning their own spouses or children, as if he might resent them for having what fate had taken from him.

She wondered how much worse it would have been if he had come alone. Would they have tried even harder to make up for Heather's absence, making the situation even more uncomfortable than it was?

As reluctant as she was to admit it, he had been smart to bring someone with him. And considering everything, she supposed she had been the right one to ask, since she understood his predicament so well. But she still thought her original idea had been the best one—to send his regrets and skip this whole reunion thing.

"You might have told me," Nic said when she and Joel were in his car again, headed for the football game, "that I was wearing the colors of your team's rival."

He gave her a ruefully apologetic look. "Sorry. I honestly didn't remember what their colors are."

Resigning herself to being seen by the home crowd as a representative of the enemy team, Nic pushed a hand through her hair and settled back into her seat. At least she liked football; she was sure she would enjoy the game.

Joel's friends surrounded them at the stadium, everyone insisting on sitting together, one Watson couple on Nic's left, the other at Joel's right. Heidi sat on the bleacher bench in front of them, beside her necessarily taciturn husband. She turned frequently to chat, her attention barely on the game.

Nic did her best to watch the plays, but it wasn't easy when everyone around them kept asking overly casual questions designed to elicit information about her and Joel. Heidi was the worst offender, of course, even though she was so polite about it that it would have been hard to get annoyed with her. All of her questions were phrased to seem as though she was simply trying to be gracious to Nic, showing interest in getting to know her better.

Nic answered each question briefly but civilly, giving away as little personal information as possible. As quickly as she could, she turned the subject to the game. "Your coach has an obsessive fondness for the standard I formation, doesn't he?" she commented to Joel. "Seems like he could change it up a bit more."

"He's been running that same formation since I played for him fifteen years ago," Joel replied.

"He should be using number twenty-three more. The kid's a natural running back. He's got the speed."

"That's what I've been saying," Earl agreed fervently. "Number twenty-three is my wife's nephew, Kirk. He's just a sophomore, but as soon as he gets a little better at tucking the ball more securely, he's going to be a force to reckon with. If Coach gives him the chance. Coach tends to focus on the same few players every game—the ones whose parents are the most vocal and active in the booster club, of course."

"Now, Earl, that's not fair," Heidi complained. "My Davey plays a lot, but it certainly isn't because his father and I are so active in the booster club."

Earl gave Nic a look that seemed to say, *See what I mean?*

Deciding discretion was called for, Nic said, "There's room on a winning team for a lot of talented players."

"So you know football?" Earl asked with interest. "Who's your favorite pro team?"

"Kansas City," she replied promptly.

Ernie gave a derisive hoot, leading to a spirited debate about pro football that morphed into a discussion of college teams and the much-maligned bowl-series system. The conversation was periodically interrupted when they all jumped to their feet to cheer on a good play by the Cardinals, in which Nic enthusiastically participated. By halftime, she and the Watson twins were great pals, much to Joel's apparent amusement.

"Not many women know football as well as you do," Earl told her, jerking a thumb toward the pleasantly plump woman at his other side. "Cassie would rather be hitting the flea markets and antique malls than watching a game."

His wife nodded her lightly graying brown head decisively to agree with that statement.

"I've always liked sports," Nic replied. "Comes from trying to keep up with my older brother, I guess. I felt as though I had to be as good as he was despite my smaller size."

"You play any sports now?"

"I'm on a softball team. And I play a little flag football. An occasional game of Ultimate Frisbee."

Earl looked impressed. "Yeah? So what do you do? You a P.E. teacher or something?"

"I'm a police officer for the Cabot Police Department."

"You're a cop? Hey, Ernie, did you hear that? Nic's a cop."

Ernie looked as surprised as his twin. Everyone else within hearing distance—most notably Heidi—had also turned to stare at her. As if, Nic thought, she had announced she was a circus geek or something. What was so odd about her being on the force?

"A police officer," Heidi repeated, twisting almost completely around on her bleacher seat. "I never would have guessed that of you. You're so…well, little. Isn't that a detriment in your job? Isn't it dangerous for you?"

"Not really. I'm well trained—and Cabot is a small town. Not exactly a hotbed of crime."

"You seem to be forgetting that guy who shot at you with a shotgun last month," Joel murmured.

His friends' eyes widened. "A shotgun?" Heidi repeated with a gasp.

Nic gave Joel a chiding look. "It was just loaded with rock salt. And old Mr. Barnett couldn't hit the side of a barn anyway. He didn't even come close to peppering me."

"And you…um, enjoy that work?"

Why did people keep asking her that, as if she would be crazy to admit that she was satisfied with her job? "Yes," she told Heidi firmly. "I do like it."

"Oh." Looking a little flustered now, Heidi glanced toward the football field, where self-consciously proud fathers escorted their shivering, scantily dressed daughters across the patchy grass. Seemingly relieved to seize a new topic, she trilled, "Oh, that brings back memories. I was a homecoming princess our senior year, you know. And Heather was queen—remember, Joel?"

Everyone around them went quiet as Joel murmured, "I remember."

Of course Heather had been homecoming queen, Nic thought with a sigh. And of course Heidi had brought her up again just as Joel seemed to be relaxing a bit and enjoying the present. She didn't believe Heidi was being deliberately cruel, simply clinging to the treasured memories of her high school days—but still, the mood changed after she spoke.

Maybe Heidi realized what she had done. Swallowing visibly, she looked at Nic again. "What were homecomings like at your school, Nicole? Did you participate?"

Nic shrugged. "I was never a homecoming princess, if that's what you're asking. I was always too much of a tomboy to be interested in fancy dresses and tiaras."

And, no, she hadn't been a cheerleader. Nor had she attended college or earned a doctorate degree or become a family counselor. She had never been a striking beauty and she doubted sincerely that her classmates thought of her as perfection personified.

She rather pitied any woman who aspired to be the next Mrs. Joel Brannon. Who could possibly compete with the memory of Saint Heather?

Whether Joel sensed her discomfort or was struggling with similar feelings of his own, he quickly turned the subject back to one that made her more comfortable—sports. Nic was pleased when the Watson brothers eagerly cooperated.

Letting Heidi and the other wives talk about homecoming fashions, Nic threw herself into the conversation about football and the upcoming basketball season. She was much more comfortable talking with the guys, she assured herself. After all, she had always considered herself one of them.

Joel wondered what he had been thinking when he'd asked Nic to accompany him to his reunion. He'd been so concerned about his own dread of the event that he hadn't given enough consideration to how awkward it would be for Nic.

He'd thought that making it clear they were only friends would take some of the pressure off her while still sending a message that he had a good life now. A full life, not a sad and lonely one.

He had imagined there would be some questions about Nic and him. After all, they were both single, and she was pretty and personable. Fascinating, actually, with her straightforward manner and her spunky individuality.

Some of his old friends probably thought he was crazy for not making a move on her. Or perhaps they thought he was still too tied up in his grief to consider being with another woman.

He wondered if they would understand if he told them that his reasons for keeping a safe distance between himself and Nic were more complicated than that. After all, she had been involved with someone else when they'd met, so they became friends without considering anything more at first. And now that friendship meant so much to him that he couldn't imagine doing anything to potentially mess it up.

Besides, judging from her last boyfriend, he was hardly her type. He was downright dull compared to party-guy Brad. Settled, routine-bound, unadventurous—the very opposite of skydiving, bull-riding, extreme-sports-loving Brad.

And now he had subjected her to this—the scrutiny of his old friends, strangers to her, and his family, all of whom seemed compelled to treat her like some sort of oddity. Because she was so refreshingly different? Or simply because she was with *him?*

During the third quarter she decided she wanted

a soft drink from the concessions stand. Joel immediately offered to get it for her, but she declined, telling him she needed to stretch her legs.

"She's something else, Joel," Ernie confided when Nic was gone. "How'd you meet a cute cop, anyway?"

"She lives next door to me in Cabot," Joel reminded him. "We're neighbors and friends. She needed a break from work and I wanted company for the trip here, so she agreed to come along with me."

"So there's nothing going on between the two of you?" Earl inquired.

Aware of several pairs of ears listening for the answer to that question, Joel forced a smile. "We're friends," he repeated. "Good friends, obviously, since she was willing to accompany me to a high school reunion."

"So there's nothing…uh…?"

"Friends," Joel said firmly.

"Of course they're just friends," Heidi said with a wave of one red-tipped hand. "I could see that right away. Nicole is a lovely girl but hardly Joel's type."

Joel felt his eyebrows rise, but he bit back the obvious question. He really didn't want to get into one of those discussions with Heidi this evening.

As fond as he was of Heidi, she had a bad habit of thinking she knew what was best for everyone else. She'd told him once that she'd always fantasized about having a syndicated advice column because she thought she was pretty good at solving other people's problems. She just had a talent, she had added with no attempt at modesty.

She had contented herself with running his father's orthodontia business—and the personal lives of everyone else who worked there—serving as perpetual president of the local PTA, chairing half a dozen committees for church and social organizations and organizing periodic reunions of her high school class. Her friends tolerated her for the most part, understanding that a kind heart and good intentions lay behind her bossiness. A few people disliked her and avoided her as much as possible.

Joel liked her well enough but was secretly glad he lived in another state.

Even knowing better than to get into a debate with Heidi, he was tempted to ask exactly why she seemed so adamant that he and Nic were mismatched. Was it only because Nic was so very different than Heather? And did Heidi really believe he would look for someone exactly like Heather if he were to consider marrying again?

Nic dropped onto the bench beside him, offering him one of the two sodas she'd brought with her, and then set a bag of popcorn between them to share. Considering the timing of her appearance, Joel wondered if she had overheard Heidi's comment. If she had, he couldn't tell from her expression, which revealed nothing of her thoughts as she tossed a handful of popcorn into her mouth and turned her attention to the game again.

For some reason, Joel had to pretty much force his own gaze away from Nic's face. He assured himself that the fact that he found her much more interest-

ing than the game wasn't particularly significant—
despite what any of his friends might think.

The Danston Cardinals won by a field goal. After
cheering until they were hoarse, the home crowd
began to move toward the exits. To keep from losing
each other in the stampede, Joel and Nic held hands
on their way out of the stadium. Their progress was
slow, especially since people kept stopping Joel to
chat with him. Nic moved along patiently beside
him, buoyed by the good spirits of the home team
supporters.

She had spotted the security officers on-site, of
course. She had worked sporting events herself on
plenty of occasions. Yet there was no officer visible
when she noticed a group of perhaps ten boys, roughly
half wearing Cardinals red, the others in Pirates black
and purple, all squaring off in a shadowy corner of the
lot. She drew her hand out of Joel's loose grip.

"Great," she murmured in resignation just as one
boy took a swing at another.

It was strictly instinct that had her running
forward, right into the path of a swinging fist.

Dodging the punch with the skill of experience,
Nic grabbed the most aggressive boy by the collar
and jerked him backward. "Break it up!" she
shouted, throwing up a hand to hold off another
would-be fighter. "Now!"

The boy she was detaining surged forward when
one of the others jeered at him for being collared by
a "little lady." A moment later Nic had his arm

twisted behind him. The furious teenager winced when she pushed upward, making it very clear that what was merely discomfort now could easily become real pain.

"Keep fighting me and you're going to be eating asphalt," she advised him loudly enough to be heard over the din. She jerked upward on his arm again to punctuate the threat.

He stilled reluctantly, and by that time several other people had arrived to help break up the fight, including Joel, the Watson twins and a uniformed officer. After some stern warnings, the boys were sent on their separate ways.

Instinctively recognizing another cop, the officer chatted with Nic for a few minutes, and then Nic turned to Joel to let him know she was ready to go. Once again she was all too aware of being the center of his former classmates' attention.

She suppressed a wince as she realized how she must have looked charging into a fight and grabbing hold of a snarling teenager. She doubted very much that Heather would have reacted to the situation that way. More likely the beloved psychologist would have encouraged the boys to sit down and talk out their problems.

"Whoa, Joel," Earl teased. "You better not mess with this one. I think she could take you."

Joel didn't seem to mind the ribbing. Instead he merely laughed and said, "I have no doubt that she could. That's why I never argue with her."

Nic gave a little snort of disbelief. "Yeah, right."

Still smiling, he motioned toward his father's car. "Let's get out of here."

"We'll see you tomorrow, Joel," Heidi called after them. "Oh, and, um, you, too, Nicole."

"She could hardly contain her enthusiasm," Nic murmured beneath her breath.

"What was that?" Joel asked as he started the car.

She snapped her seat belt and gave him an artificially bright smile. "Nothing. Great game, huh?"

"Yeah. It's always nice when our team wins the homecoming game."

"Sorry if I embarrassed you by breaking up that fight. Habit kicked in, I guess."

"You didn't embarrass me." He seemed surprised that she had suggested it. "I just wish I had reacted as quickly as you did. I didn't even realize what was going on until you were already in the middle of it."

"I've worked enough ball games to know when a fight's starting."

"You handled that tall guy easily enough. Don't you ever worry that your smaller size will put you at a disadvantage?"

"I've learned to use it to my benefit. You know what they say—small but wiry. Besides, the guy was tall but skinny beneath those baggy clothes. I doubt he outweighed me by much."

He chuckled. "I don't think I'll put Earl's theory to the test anytime soon."

"Earl's theory?"

"That you could take me down. He's probably right."

Most men seemed to have a problem with the idea of being bested in a physical confrontation by a woman. Brad, for one, had always had a need to prove himself around Nic, challenging her to foot and bike races and other endurance tests. Even friendly games of pool and darts had become fierce competitions when the two of them had gone head-to-head.

It was almost as if the subtext had been, *You might be a trained officer of the law, but I'm the real man in the relationship.* Nic had gotten the message, but she hadn't backed down—and in some ways, Brad had respected that. Until he'd gotten tired of it, of course, and gone looking for someone with whom he didn't have to work quite so hard at maintaining his ego.

If Joel harbored any similar feelings of threatened masculinity, he hid them very well. He cheerfully admitted that he was no fighter and that his idea of extreme sports was a rousing game of racquetball in the local gym. He had no problems being friends with a woman who could hold her own in a physical contest—but she didn't know how he would feel about being in a romantic relationship with a woman like her.

As far as she knew, he'd had only a few dates during the time she had known him, usually when he had needed a companion for some social function he had been expected to attend in his position as one of Cabot's prominent professionals. His choices had been fairly predictable, as far as Nic was concerned. A pretty kindergarten teacher who'd once been a Miss Arkansas runner-up. An attractive divorcée who owned a successful travel agency. A veterinarian from nearby Searcy that he had met through mutual friends.

If there had been any second dates with any of them, Nic wasn't aware of it. She had always believed—and Aislinn concurred—that Joel had deliberately refrained from leading any woman on to believe he was interested in more than a pleasant evening of companionship. The more she learned about his late wife, the more she could understand how difficult it was for him to find anyone who measured up to her.

Vaguely depressed—or maybe she was just tired—she leaned back in the plush seat of Dr. Lou Brannon's sedan and pretended to listen to the music streaming from the stereo speakers.

Chapter Five

Elaine was in the den, sipping a cup of what smelled like herbal tea and watching the evening news on TV, when Nic and Joel returned from the game. She wore a floor-length pink velveteen robe that revealed just a hint of a lacy white nightgown at the neck, making her resemblance to a porcelain doll even more striking to Nic.

Smiling when they walked into the room, she asked, "How was the game?"

Joel leaned down to brush a kiss against his mother's cheek. "We won. By a late-game field goal. Very exciting."

"Oh, I'm glad. And your reunion? How did that go?"

"It was nice enough. I wish it were over."

Elaine shook her head. "And skip the big event tomorrow evening? Heidi would be heartbroken. She's been planning this for months."

Joel sighed heavily. "Yeah, I know. I'm just not particularly looking forward to it."

"You could always have an emergency call from Cabot," Nic suggested helpfully. "You've made your appearance and proven to everyone that you're okay. They wouldn't be surprised if a busy doctor had to bail early."

Joel seemed to consider the suggestion, but Elaine shook her head in disapproval. "Lie to your old friends?" she asked. "People who have been so looking forward to seeing you? I'm sure you're only teasing, Nicole, but Joel would never do that."

Giving Nic a wry look that let her know he was well aware she hadn't been teasing, Joel appeased his mother by saying, "I'll go to the party, Mom. And I'll probably even have a pretty good time. But that doesn't mean I'm counting the minutes until it starts."

Still frowning a little in Nic's direction, Elaine rose from the couch. "I think I'll turn in. Your father already went up, since he was tired from a particularly long day. Can I walk you to your bedroom, Nicole?"

Startled by the offer, Nic shook her head. "Thanks, but I'll go up in a little while. I think I'll watch a little TV first to wind down from the game, if that's okay."

"Of course it's okay," Joel assured her. "Actually,

I need to wind down a little myself. Maybe have a cup of that herbal tea Mom's been drinking."

"All right." Elaine looked somewhat anxiously from Nic to Joel and back. "You'll let us know if you need anything during the night, Nicole?"

"I'll be fine. Good night, Mrs. Brannon."

"Yes. Good night."

Nic waited until she was sure the older woman was out of earshot before she turned to Joel. "Did she really think I'd jump you as soon as we were alone together?"

Joel blinked a couple of times in surprise at her blunt question, but then he smiled and shook his head. "Why on earth would you think that?"

"It was obvious that she didn't want to leave us in here together."

"I'm sure you're imagining things. Mom's kind of hard to read sometimes."

Nic didn't think Elaine was at all hard to read. To her, it was clear that Elaine had come to the conclusion that Nic was not a suitable match for her son. Perhaps she thought Nic was angling to be the next Mrs. Brannon.

Elaine was probably convinced that any woman in her right mind would be interested in snagging her good-looking, successful-doctor son. Especially, Nic thought cynically, a woman like her—an average-looking small-town cop nearing her thirties.

A woman who couldn't be more opposite from the daughter-in-law Elaine had obviously adored.

Dismissing the comments about his mother's

motives, Joel motioned Nic toward the couch. "Make yourself comfortable. You want something to drink? A nightcap? Soda? Hot cocoa?"

"Hot cocoa sounds good, actually. Can I help you with it?"

"No, sit tight. I'll get it. Marshmallows or whipped cream?"

"Marshmallows, of course." Sinking onto the deep, comfortable, intimidatingly white sofa cushions, Nic reached for the remote control. Might as well watch Letterman's Top Ten since she was up, she figured.

Her cell phone rang while a local car dealer was shouting at the camera about the crazy deals he was offering for the month of October. Hearing the familiar opening refrains of her personalized ringtone—The Beatles' "Here Comes the Sun"— she scrambled in the canvas tote bag she used for a purse to find the small phone.

Aislinn's number was displayed on the screen. Surprised—and a little concerned—Nic held the phone to her ear. "Aislinn? What's wrong?"

"That's what I was going to ask you," her friend said somberly. "Are you okay?"

"I'm fine. Why do you ask?"

"I don't know. I just had a feeling that something was wrong there. Something involving you."

"Well, your feeling is misguided for once. Everything is perfectly fine here. Joel and I just got back from the football game, and the home team won and everything. Joel's old friend's were nice, for the most part, and I had a pretty good time, considering that I was attending someone else's reunion."

"So there was no…?"

"No what?" Nic prodded patiently.

"For some reason, I had a feeling you were in some sort of danger. Silly, I know, but…well, I had to call."

Nic couldn't help but smile. Aislinn could deny all she wanted that she had psychic abilities, but if she had picked up on the minor incident tonight, her abilities were much stronger than she wanted to admit.

"There was a fight after the game between some of the rival schoolkids. Well, almost a fight. I got in the middle of it and broke it up, along with some help from Joel and his friends and a security officer. It might have turned ugly if we hadn't been there to stop it, but it was over almost before it began. I was never in danger."

"A fight, huh?" Aislinn was quiet for a few minutes, as if trying to make the facts fit with her feelings.

"I suppose that could be it," she conceded eventually, though she still sounded hesitant. "You weren't hurt or anything, were you?"

"Not even a scratch. They were just kids—and skinny ones, at that."

"Okay. Good. So you're having a good time?"

"Let's just say I'm not ready to slit my wrists. Yet."

Aislinn laughed. "I'll take that as a good sign. What are you doing now? Did I get you out of bed?"

"No, Joel and I were just about to have some hot chocolate. Actually, here he is now." She smiled up at him as he stood over her, two steaming, marshmallow-topped mugs in his hands. "Aislinn says hi."

"Tell her hi back. She checking to see if you've bolted yet?"

"Pretty much. Joel says hi, Aislinn."

"I'll let you enjoy your cocoa. Have fun tomorrow. And, Nic…be careful, okay?"

"Yeah, sure. Of course. You know me, I'm always careful."

"Right." Aislinn didn't sound overly confident when she disconnected.

"What was that all about?" Joel asked as he handed Nic her mug, then sank onto the couch beside her.

Nic dropped her phone back into her tote bag and shrugged. "With Aislinn, who knows? She had a feeling that I was in danger, so she had to call."

"In danger? Here?" The slight alarm in Joel's expression was an indication of how seriously he had learned to take Aislinn's vague warnings. "What did she say?"

Licking marshmallow off her lip, Nic shook her head reassuringly. "I told her about the fight we broke up at the ballpark. She agreed that was probably what had set off her…well, her intuition or whatever the heck it is that gives her those feelings. She felt a lot better after I told her how minor the whole thing was."

"So she somehow picked up that you were in the middle of a fight earlier and she felt compelled to call and make sure you were okay."

"Yeah. Basically." Nic took another sip of her cocoa, enjoying the rich taste as it slid across her tongue.

"You have odd friends, Nic."

She laughed. "You can say that after we just spent the evening with Heidi and the Watson twins?"

Looking rueful, Joel nodded. "Okay, you've got a point there."

"You make really good cocoa. This is delicious."

Smiling, he reached out to smooth a bit of marshmallow off her lip with the ball of his thumb. "It's a mix. Add boiling water and stir."

For some reason, she was suddenly flustered. She cleared her throat, looked into her mug and babbled, "No kidding? It's better than the mixes I buy."

Joel's voice sounded a little strained when he replied. "Mom makes it herself using powdered milk and cocoa and stuff. I don't know what else is in it. A little cinnamon, I think."

"Maybe she'll give me the recipe before we leave."

"I'm sure she would be delighted."

Talk of his mother had changed the mood between them. Joel didn't comment when Nic scooted a couple inches farther away from him on the couch, setting her mug on a coaster on the end table as an excuse for the change of position. Just to keep things comfortable, she turned up the television a bit, focusing her attention on the screen.

Pretending to be checking for the remains of melted marshmallow, she ran her fingertips across her lips— lingering just for a moment at the spot Joel had touched.

* * *

After setting their cocoa mugs in the dishwasher and turning off the TV, Joel walked Nic up to the guest room for the night.

"You're sure there's nothing else you need tonight?"

She smiled up at him. "No, I'm good. Thanks."

"I'm right next door if you need anything."

She glanced automatically in the direction he had indicated. His bedroom door looked awfully close to her own. "Not very far," she murmured.

"No." He looked from his door to hers, then gave her a weak smile. "Not far at all."

"So...um...good night, Joel."

"Good night, Nic."

He didn't immediately move away. He just stood there looking down at her. And suddenly her heart was beating so hard in her chest that she could hardly breathe. Feeling an uncharacteristic heat flood her cheeks, she took a quick step backward, swinging the door closed between them.

What, she asked herself, was *that?*

Joel threw his Cardinal-red polo shirt over the back of a chair and pushed his hand through his tousled hair. For some reason, he was restless tonight. Itchy.

Must be the reunion making him feel that way, he mused. The reminders of his younger self, the signs of aging in all his friends—signs he assumed they were also seeing in him. He supposed it was only natural to feel nostalgic for the more innocent and carefree days of his youth when he was around the people who had shared those times with him.

And yet…oddly enough, he wasn't thinking of those old days now. He found his thoughts turning more to the life he had made for himself in Arkansas—his home, his patients, his friends. Especially the one friend now sleeping only a few steps down the hall.

Despite his vague feelings of guilt earlier for subjecting her to this ordeal, he was glad he had brought her. Having Nic with him had made the whole evening so much easier, giving him an excuse to avoid discussing Heather's death with his former classmates, keeping him grounded in the present. Not to mention that he simply enjoyed being with Nic.

Remembering the enthusiasm with which she had cheered on his high school team, he couldn't help but smile. Nic wasn't exactly shy and retiring. She had impressed the heck out of the Watson twins with her knowledge of football. And she was hardly a high-maintenance companion. She didn't expect him to constantly entertain her or cater to her needs. In fact, she was firmly insistent upon taking care of herself, not even letting him go to the concession stand for her snacks.

His smile faded a little when he recalled the way she had waded into that potential brawl in the stadium parking lot. When most other women—and most men, for that matter—would have stayed safely at a distance, doing nothing more to help than looking for the nearest officer, Nic had simply taken matters into her own hands. It hadn't even seemed to occur to her that the angry teenagers almost all dwarfed her in size.

He still didn't understand why his old friends seemed to think she was a little odd. Because she was a police officer? Female police officers might still be in the minority, but they were hardly a rarity these days.

Because she liked football? Again, hardly a big deal. He knew a lot of women who liked sports. His nurse was the biggest NASCAR fan he knew, quoting statistics and rankings that could make his head spin with confusion.

Because she hadn't even hesitated about throwing herself into that fight? They should admire her for that. He was a bit chagrined that it had taken him so long to intervene himself. Had Nic not been there, one of those kids could have gotten hurt before anyone had had the presence of mind to break them up.

He kept coming back to the suspicion that it was simply that Nic was so different from Heather. And again he thought that was a really lame reason why he and Nic couldn't be good friends—or even more, if they had chosen to pursue anything else.

Now he was all itchy again, thinking incongruously of Nic standing in the doorway of her bedroom, gazing up at him with what might have been an uncharacteristic hint of nerves in her big dark blue eyes. Had that been just a touch of a blush on her smooth, soft-looking cheeks? Had she, too, been struck by the intimacy of saying good-night in a quiet, darkened house in which they would both be sleeping tonight? Or was it all in his own imagination?

Maybe bringing Nic to his reunion hadn't been such a good idea after all, he thought, throwing himself onto his old double bed. Their friendship meant entirely too much to him for him to take any chance at all on putting a new distance between them.

It was always awkward to wake up in a strange house, disheveled and disoriented. Pushing her tousled hair out of her face, Nic gathered her clothes and makeup bag and opened the bedroom door. The hallway was empty and the house was quiet, making her wonder if she was the only one awake at seven o'clock on this Saturday.

She had just reached the bathroom door when it opened. Wearing only a pair of jeans and rubbing a towel over his wet hair, Joel stepped out, almost walking straight into her. He stopped abruptly when he realized she was there. "Whoa. Sorry, I didn't mean to run you down."

"You didn't," she assured him, stepping quickly backward. "I didn't know you were in there."

"I'm done. It's all yours now. Do you need anything?"

"I, um…" For some reason, her mind had suddenly gone blank. She couldn't even remember exactly what he had asked. She had known that he was fit, of course, in a sturdy, solid-looking way—but who knew there were such serious muscles hidden beneath his conservative-young-professional clothing?

"Nic?"

He was looking at her oddly, and she forced her attention away from his pecs and abs. "Sorry. I guess I'm not completely awake yet. What did you say?"

"I asked if you need anything. Soap, shampoo and towels are all laid out for you in there, but if there's anything else…"

"No, I've got everything. Thanks."

Nodding, he moved toward his bedroom. A moment later he looked inquiringly over his shoulder. "Problem?"

Starting, she shook her head and ducked into the bathroom, closing the door a bit too sharply behind her. She really hoped he had believed her lame excuse about still being sleep-addled. She would hate to think he suspected she'd been watching him walk away and wondering if those pants concealed an equally impressive physique.

It must be something in the Alabama air, she thought as she plunged beneath the showerhead into water that was just warm enough to be tolerable. She hadn't been acting quite like herself ever since she and Joel had arrived here.

Showered, blow-dried, made-up and dressed in a cropped denim jacket over a lace-trimmed camisole and boot-cut jeans with short brown leather boots, Nic decided she was as presentable as she was going to be to start this second day of Joel's reunion. She had given more attention to her appearance than she usually did, even running a bit of styling gel through her somewhat shaggily layered dark blond hair. She was wearing eyeliner, for Pete's sake.

She told herself that she had taken such care with her grooming because it was only courteous to look her best for a gathering of Joel's old friends. Her hostess was obviously into that sort of thing, judging by Elaine's meticulous hairstyle and makeup, and Nic wouldn't want to look grubby in Joel's mother's eyes.

Not that she was competing with anyone, she assured herself as she started down the stairs. Not with Elaine or Heidi—and certainly not with anyone's memory of a beautiful redhead.

She had expected to find Joel downstairs with his parents. Instead the living room and dining room were empty. Following a few muted sounds into the kitchen, Nic found Elaine pouring batter into a waffle iron.

Elaine smiled brightly when Nic entered. "Good morning. I'm making Belgian waffles with fresh-sliced strawberries and whipped cream. But if you'd rather have eggs or oatmeal…"

"I love Belgian waffles," Nic assured her. "But you shouldn't have gone to so much trouble for my sake."

Shaking her head, which didn't ruffle a hair of her perfectly curled and firmly sprayed coif, Elaine took a carafe of orange juice—fresh-squeezed, no doubt—from the refrigerator and set it on the counter. "It's no trouble at all. Joel loves waffles, so I always make them when he's home. Not that he comes home all that often," she added with a little frown.

"He stays really busy in Cabot," Nic said, feeling a need to come to Joel's defense. "He works ten hours a day, five days a week, and usually puts in a couple of hours on Saturdays and Sundays. And he makes himself available to his patients even when he isn't working, voluntarily staying on call almost 24-7."

Rather than appeasing Joel's mother about his reasons for not visiting more often, Nic's comments seemed to only worry her more. "I worry about him working that hard. He's going to burn out. Or get sick."

"He seems to enjoy it," Nic offered weakly. "He loves the kids."

Elaine sighed heavily as she stacked perfectly browned waffles on a serving platter. "He always has loved children. He and Heather planned to have several of their own."

"Is there anything I can do to help you, Mrs. Brannon?" Nic asked, hoping to change the subject.

Rousing herself from her melancholy memories, Elaine motioned toward the juice pitcher. "You can set that on the table in the breakfast nook if you'd like. I'm almost finished here."

Nic carried the pitcher around the bar that separated the well-appointed kitchen from the breakfast nook set into a bay window that overlooked the sizable, neatly landscaped backyard. Spotting movement at the back of the yard, Nic noticed that Joel and his father were walking the perimeter, apparently examining the redwood fence that surrounded the property.

"Are you having problems with your fence?" she asked Elaine more to make small talk than because she was particularly interested.

Elaine shook her head in exasperation. "Lou is obsessed with termites. He's convinced they're going to attack at any moment, even though we have regular inspections by professionals. Nearly every time one of the boys comes over, he makes them help him look for signs of termite invasion."

Nic found that amusing, though she noticed that Joel seemed to be taking the task very seriously. She watched as he bent to brush a few dried leaves away from the bottom of the fence, and her attention lingered for a moment on the way the morning sun brought out the gold highlights in his light brown hair.

Elaine set the platter of waffles on the round cherry table with a thump that might have been a bit more forceful than necessary. "Do you drink coffee, Nicole?" she asked, bringing Nic's attention back inside.

Nic couldn't help but wonder if that had been Elaine's intention.

Chapter Six

Telling herself she was reading hidden agendas into perfectly innocent actions, Nic turned away from the window and smiled at Joel's mother. "Yes, I drink coffee. Cops tend to pretty much live on caffeine and fast food."

Elaine had already returned to the kitchen, where she poured steaming coffee into a delicate flowered cup. "It must be difficult being a woman in such a traditionally male occupation."

"Not so much anymore. I'm not the only woman in my department, though we are outnumbered. Thanks," she added as Elaine handed her the cup.

"Do you plan to keep working in the police force even after you marry and have children?"

It was a question straight out of the last century, especially when combined with Elaine's tone and expression. Nic tried to answer it with a smile. "I haven't really thought about it. And it isn't an issue now, since I don't expect to get married or have children anytime soon."

"Oh? You don't want children?"

It took an effort, but Nic managed to keep her smile steady. "Not at the moment."

"You're—what?—twenty-six?"

"Twenty-seven. This coffee is really good. What brand do you use?"

Either Elaine hadn't heard the question or she did a good job of pretending. "I had two boys by the time I was your age. Our little Kyle was born a month before my thirtieth birthday."

Nic's mild irritation immediately evaporated. "Joel told me about Kyle," she said gently. "I was sorry to hear about your loss. I know it must be very painful for you still."

Though her eyes held a world of old pain, Elaine kept her face serene. "Thank you, dear. It was a terrible trial for us, but we're a close family. We found comfort in each other, just as we did when we lost our Heather five and a half years ago."

Our Heather. What sort of message was Elaine sending with that phrasing? Or was Nic only imagining that there was a message?

"I have an older brother myself," she volunteered. "My mother and I leaned on him quite a bit when my father died a few years ago. Mother is living with him now in Europe, where he works for a U.S. embassy. It's nice to have family to turn to when you need them."

What might have been a glimmer of approval appeared in the look Elaine gave her then. "Yes, it is."

Feeling as if she had just scored a hard-earned point—even though she wasn't quite sure of the rules in this particular game—Nic took another sip of her coffee.

She was immeasurably relieved when the kitchen door opened and Joel and Lou came into the kitchen along with a draft of cool October air. "Is breakfast ready?" Joel wanted to know, smiling from his mother to Nic. "I'm starving."

Her voice going practically liquid with doting affection, Elaine patted Joel's arm and replied, "Everything's ready. Seat your guest and then take your own chair. I'll get your coffee."

"Yes, ma'am." Sharing a look with Nic, Joel made a production of holding a chair for her.

Feeling a bit foolish, Nic sank into it and reached for the napkin—snowy linen—that sat beside the flowered plate Elaine had already laid ready on a crisp yellow linen place mat.

The stack of waffles disappeared quickly. Other than murmuring a few compliments about the delicious food, Nic said little during the meal, listening quietly as the others talked about local people and events. Joel made an occasional attempt to include her in the discussion, but she answered in polite monosyllables, sending the conversational ball back into their court.

"I thought Ethan might join us for breakfast this morning," Joel said as he pushed his empty plate away and reached for his freshly refilled coffee cup.

Lou frowned. "Ethan's been pretty busy lately. He's involved in some project he hasn't discussed with us. He said he'd tell us about it when he's ready to talk about it."

"What does Ethan do?" Nic asked.

"He's an independent financial consultant," Joel answered. "Basically he goes into small businesses that are struggling to make it and he helps them turn a profit."

"So he's like a financial genius?"

Joel chuckled. "You could say that. He'd hate it, but you could say it."

"I suppose it's true enough when you're talking about other people's money," Lou complained. "You couldn't say it applied to himself. He doesn't charge enough for his services, and I've been telling him that for years. With his talents, he should be a wealthy man by now. Instead he's just getting by."

"He makes enough for his needs," Elaine responded loyally. "He's promised me he's putting enough away for his future, but he says he doesn't need any more than he brings in now. Ethan isn't interested in amassing a fortune just to impress other people."

"It isn't a matter of impressing people, it's a matter of security. Someday he might find a woman who'll look beyond that difficult exterior of his and actually want to start a family with him and then he'll wish he had planned a little better for his own needs rather than all these small-business owners he works with every day."

From Lou's tone, Nic got the impression that this was an old argument and one he no longer expected to win. Lou was fond of both his sons, that was obvious, but he acted almost as though he blamed himself that their lives hadn't turned out exactly as he and Elaine had hoped and planned for them. Apparently they thought Ethan should be a wealthy business consultant with a suitable wife and children, and that Joel should be running an upscale metropolitan pediatrics clinic—and still married to the woman they had all loved.

It seemed to her that they should be more proud of the men their sons had become. Decent, hardworking men with a purpose—to help others rather than amassing fortunes for themselves. But then, the Brannon family dynamics were none of her business. She was only here for another few hours, and then it was entirely likely she would never see them again.

Except for Joel, of course. As her neighbor and friend, he would continue to be an important part of her life.

Perhaps Elaine decided they were revealing too much in front of a guest. Her voice was almost chirpy when she asked, "So what exactly are your plans for today, Joel? I know your class party doesn't start until six o'clock, so that gives you several hours free this morning."

"Heidi has arranged golf and tennis tournaments at the resort and a spa day for the women who were interested, but Nic and I decided to pass on those activities. I thought I'd give her a tour of the area, if she's interested. Show her some of the local highlights."

"I'd love that." Nic's enthusiasm had more to do with getting out of the house than sightseeing. And she'd just about rather eat bugs than participate in a spa day with Heidi and the other wives.

Joel probably knew exactly what she was thinking, but he merely smiled and said, "Great. Dad, you mind if we borrow your car again?"

"Not at all. I was going to spend the day working in the yard anyway. Got to get those leaves raked up."

"And I have a meeting at the church," Elaine said. "Fay's picking me up, so your father can use my car if he needs to go anywhere. Why don't we all meet back here for cocktails before you leave for your party? Say, five o'clock?"

"Sure. We'll have to change for the party anyway," Joel agreed with a shrug.

"Let me help you clear away the breakfast dishes," Nic offered, reaching for the empty waffle platter.

Elaine shook her head firmly. "You and Joel go have fun," she insisted. "I really prefer to take care of things in my kitchen by myself, though I appreciate your offer."

"We gave up trying to help in the kitchen a long time ago," Joel said with a grin. "Mom has her particular way of doing things and she doesn't like anyone messing up her system."

"She did let Heather help her some," Lou reminisced. "But she was training Heather to do things her way."

Joel's chair scraped on the floor when he shoved it back from the table. "Since we're forbidden to help with the cleaning up, maybe we should just go," he said to Nic. "I'll take you down to see the revitalized historic town square."

She sprang to her feet. "Sounds fascinating."

There wasn't a lot to see in Danston. The driving tour took just over an hour, and that included looking at the old courthouse twice.

Joel had driven slowly, doing the tour-guide thing by pointing out places that had been significant to him growing up. The high school. The drugstore with the old-fashioned soda fountain where he and his friends had hung out after school. Though the drugstore was still in business, the soda fountain had closed several years ago, leaving the teenagers to gather in the chain fast-food restaurants in the newer part of town.

The two-screen movie theater where he had watched the teen comedies of the eighties had been replaced by a six-screen stadium-seating multiplex out on the highway. The old roller-skating rink was gone now, and several of the mom-and-pop stores had closed when the big-box superstore opened just off the highway, next to the new theater. But as Joel had said, downtown was being revitalized with an influx of shops selling antiques, gifts, crafts and specialty items like kitchen gadgets and bath supplies.

Nic admired the old-fashioned street lamps that lined the newly resurfaced sidewalks and the facades of old buildings that had been given facelifts. "It's a nice town," she said. "I'll bet people come from all over to shop on the square."

He nodded. "Especially at Christmas. The downtown merchants go all out decorating for the holidays with lights and window displays and garlands—keeping everything old-fashioned and pedestrian-friendly. It's really nice then. You should see it."

Nic thought the chances of her ever visiting here at Christmas were remote, but she kept that thought to herself as she answered, "It sounds great."

"Yeah. It's nice."

That subject exhausted, he turned the car at an intersection and drove in silence for several long moments. Nic tried to think of something to say to fill the gap. "I know you haven't been home for a while to visit. If you'd like to spend more time with your parents today, don't feel like you need to entertain me. I packed a couple of books and I'd be perfectly comfortable reading in your mom's living room while you visit with them."

"To be honest, I'd rather spend most of the day out with you. I love my parents, Nic, I really do, but spending too much time with them is kind of stressful. For all of us, I think."

Nic lifted an eyebrow. "Why?"

Keeping his eyes on the increasingly rural road ahead, he shrugged. "I don't know, exactly. They still don't understand why I wanted to move away. I guess we've all just grown apart some during the past five or six years."

Since Heather's death, Nic thought with a slight shake of her head. She knew that tragedies tended to either bring families closer together or push them apart. Elaine had said that losing little Kyle had brought them closer, but Heather's death seemed to have had the opposite effect.

"Where are we going now?" she asked, since she was no expert in family dynamics—as Heather had been, she remembered with a wince.

"I thought I'd show you where Ethan lives. He's got a place near the river outside of town. A dam was built back in the fifties to create the lake. Lake Parnell, named after an old local family. Ethan lives about five miles upriver from the dam.

"The lakeside resort where most of the reunion guests from out of town are staying and where we'll meet for the dance tonight is called the Parnell Resort and Conference Center. It used to be an old fishing lodge, but it was remodeled during this past summer to update all the guest rooms and add the ballroom and some conference rooms. There aren't many conferences held around here, of course, but several of the local civic organizations will use the facilities for monthly meetings and fund-raisers and such."

Figuring he was pretty much looking for any excuse to keep from returning home, and going back into tour-guide mode to keep from talking about why, she nodded and sat back in her seat to watch the pastoral scenery passing on the other side of the glass.

Ethan's home was hardly luxurious, but Nic could certainly see why he would want to live there. A cedar-sided cabin with big windows and a small yard, his house sat close enough to the riverbank that he could easily throw a rock from his back door into the water. He had a no-frills boat dock with a tin-roofed shelter for his fishing boat and a cedar-shake-topped gazebo over a concrete picnic table and a stone barbecue. It looked more like a weekend fishing cabin than a full-time residence, but she supposed Ethan liked the rustic solitude.

"It's nice."

Joel nodded. "Yeah. I've spent occasional weekends here with him. We fish, watch TV, eat grilled meat."

"Have long brotherly talks?"

Chuckling, Joel shook his head. "Ethan's not one for talking much."

"He's never been married?"

"Nope. Says no one can put up with him long enough. The truth is, of course, that he won't compromise enough to make it work with anyone."

Wrinkling her nose, Nic murmured, "I guess it's no surprise that I can identify with that."

"No surprise at all," Joel replied with a laugh. "Ethan's truck is in the driveway. Want to stop and say hi while we're here?"

"He doesn't mind drop-in visits?"

"Nah. Ethan doesn't really care about social niceties. If he wants to see us, he'll ask us in. If not, he'll tell us he's busy and send us on our way."

The affectionate tolerance in Joel's tone kept the comments from being critical. He didn't seem to find anything particularly odd in Ethan's behavior; perhaps because he was simply so accustomed to it.

He parked behind Ethan's older-model brown pickup and opened his door. Nic didn't wait for him to come around to open hers. She stepped out into the crisp—but not cold—October air and inhaled the scent of fresh country air. Even the atmosphere was peaceful here, with little traffic on the road and no neighbors in direct line of sight.

"It reminds me of my uncle's fishing cabin on the Buffalo River," she said as she and Joel moved toward the front porch that held two redwood rockers and a chain-suspended redwood swing. "I used to love going there with my family for Labor Day."

"My grandfather used to have a place similar to this in Michigan. We would go there when we went to visit when we were kids. Granddad died when I was ten and we haven't been back since, but Ethan always said he was going to live in a fishing cabin someday. As soon as he had the money, he built this place."

Filing that tidbit away with the few other items she knew about Joel's older brother, Nic watched as Joel tapped lightly on his brother's front door. It opened almost immediately, making her wonder if Ethan had heard them drive up.

Ethan smiled when he saw his brother standing at his door. Nic thought about how much more approachable he looked when he smiled. No matter how often people commented about his occasional grumpiness, he seemed to be a pretty decent guy underneath. Still, his smile changed again when he turned to her, and she wondered what it was about her that bothered him.

"Nic," he said perfectly politely. "It's good to see you again. Are you enjoying your visit to Danston?"

"Very much. Joel's been giving me a tour of the area."

Ethan chuckled. "That must not have taken long. Come on in. I'll make a pot of coffee."

Apparently he was feeling social today. Nic followed Joel into the house, discreetly studying the decor on her way in. She wasn't particularly surprised to see that Ethan's tastes ran to minimalist comfort. Deep couches and chairs, functional tables, a big rock fireplace, built-in shelving, few knick-knacks or wall decorations.

It was a man's place, a bachelor's home, and Ethan was probably quite comfortable living here. She couldn't help wondering, though, if he had ever wished for someone to share it with.

The kitchen was especially inviting, with its big windows, industrial-looking appliances and a hanging rack that held well-used-looking copper-bottomed pans. "You like to cook?" she asked Ethan in some surprise.

He shrugged. "I like to eat. I don't like frozen dinners or fast food and I live too far out of town for deliveries or takeout. I had to learn to cook."

"Very practical."

"He's a great cook, actually," Joel volunteered. "Especially if you happen to be a carnivore."

"Have y'all had lunch?" Ethan asked. "We could put some burgers on the grill."

Because Joel seemed to like the idea, Nic agreed that it sounded like fun. And it turned out that she was right. Preparing and eating lunch with the Brannon brothers was a pleasant way to spend a couple of hours.

She enjoyed watching the interaction between them, making note of their differences—and their similarities. Despite the fact that Ethan wasn't much of a gabber, he and Joel talked easily enough, sharing a sort of fraternal shorthand that left Nic occasionally confused but never feeling deliberately excluded.

Ethan seemed particularly interested in hearing about Nic's work.

"It's not exactly nonstop excitement," she replied in answer to his questions. "I work a lot of traffic accidents, standard break-ins, domestic disputes, that sort of thing."

"You carry a weapon. Have you ever had to discharge it?"

"Not in the line of duty. I practice regularly on the shooting range to make sure I'll be prepared if I ever have to open fire."

"She's used her Taser a couple times," Joel said, wiping his fingers on a paper napkin. "Even had it used on her. She showed me the videotape of the experience."

"It's standard procedure for officers who are trained at using the Taser to have it used on them," Nic explained when Ethan turned a questioning look her way. "That way we know firsthand what we're inflicting on other people."

"What's it like?"

"Pure hell," she answered without hesitation. "It doesn't last long in actuality, but it feels like forever while you're being hit with that voltage. I went down to my knees. But I stayed conscious," she added proudly.

Ethan's smile was wry. "Congratulations."

"It's actually a very effective weapon despite the inevitable controversy about its use. A nonlethal method of controlling situations that have the potential to flare out of control."

Ethan had a few more questions, which she answered patiently. At least he was talking to her now, and the earlier suspicion in his eyes was fading when he looked at her. Maybe he'd realized from watching her and Joel together that they really were just friends. That Nic had no particular designs on Joel.

Apparently he was fine with her as Joel's friend; he just had concerns about her being more. Even though it wasn't an issue, she couldn't help but wonder why he didn't want her to get too close to Joel.

Chapter Seven

They had finished lunch and were just beginning to clear away the remains when they were all startled by the opening notes of the Scooby Doo theme music. Smiling sheepishly, Joel reached for his belt. "My phone," he said.

Ethan rolled his eyes. "What ever happened to phones that simply ring?" he asked rhetorically.

Ignoring his brother, Joel had already taken the call. "Have you tested her blood-glucose levels?" he asked, walking into the other room with a motion to indicate he would return soon.

"He really is always on call, isn't he?" Ethan commented, still looking toward the doorway through which Joel had disappeared.

"Yes, he is. And he doesn't resent it in the least. I've never seen anyone love his work as much as Joel does."

Ethan shrugged and reached for Joel's empty plate. "The work's pretty much all he's got."

Nic felt her eyebrows rise. "Is that what you really think?"

"Well, you know, he doesn't have many hobbies. And since, er…"

"Since Heather died," Nic supplied in resignation.

"Well, yeah. He's pretty much focused exclusively on work since then."

Carrying a pile of dishes to the counter, Nic shook her head. "Did you know Joel sometimes teaches a kids' Sunday school class back in Cabot? Or that he plays racquetball with friends twice a week? Or that he paints some absolutely beautiful watercolors?"

Looking startled, Ethan set his load of flatware on the counter and stared at her. "Joel does watercolors? I mean, he used to like to mess around with colored pencils and stuff when he was in school, but—"

"But you have no idea what he likes now," she finished with a disapproving shake of her head. "You know what, Ethan? I think you and your family and pretty much this whole town have frozen Joel in some sort of time warp. To all of you, he's still that golden boy from high school or the grieving widower from five years ago. You can't seem to see that he's matured and moved on."

"And you're judging this on the basis of…what?

Not quite twelve hours with us?" Ethan's tone was just a bit too polite, giving her a hint that her assessment had irked him.

She wasn't in the least intimidated despite his frown, which might have made a more timid woman quail. "Not just that. I've known Joel for almost a year, remember? Living next door to him, I've seen him almost every day during that time, spent quite a bit of time talking with him. I couldn't help noticing that you've never visited him there."

Ethan's scowl deepened, and she wasn't sure whether he was more annoyed or chagrined, though she saw both emotions in his expression. "He hasn't invited me."

She tilted her head. "Your parents, either?"

"No. Not really. When he wants to visit, he comes here. He has never suggested that we go there."

Interesting. Was Joel making a deliberate effort to keep his new life in Arkansas separate from his past here in Alabama? "Maybe he's waiting for you to express interest in visiting him there."

"Maybe." But Ethan didn't sound convinced.

She could still hear Joel talking in the other room as she rinsed a glass and set it in the dishwasher. "He really is doing fine, Ethan. He's happy, his practice is thriving, he has friends. There's no need for everyone to look so worried about him."

A muscle tightened in Ethan's jaw. "You didn't see him before," he muttered. "After—"

Nic was beginning to feel frustrated that no one

around here seemed to be able to say the words. "After Heather died."

Ethan nodded, his throat working with a visible swallow.

Maybe Nic had watched too many television movies-of-the-week—the ones that often seemed to feature men in love with their brothers' wives. Something in Ethan's expression made her wonder....

Oblivious to the somber conversation they had been having about him, Joel strolled back into the kitchen with an apologetic expression. "Sorry. I told Mrs. Carpenter to call me if she had any concerns about her daughter this weekend."

"I hope nothing's terribly wrong?" Nic said.

"No. We just need to make an adjustment to her meds. She'll be fine."

Nic hoped Ethan noticed how fulfilling Joel found his work despite the occasional interruption of his personal life. It was so obvious to her that Joel hadn't minded the call at all—just the opposite, in fact.

"Anyway," Joel continued, "I hope you two didn't mind me taking a call during our visit."

"Of course not," Nic replied for them both with a dismissive wave of her hand. And then she smiled for Joel's benefit. "At least it wasn't Aislinn again with another foreboding feeling."

"That's true. I could start getting worried if she called again."

"Aislinn?" Ethan inquired, wondering about the inside joke.

Joel chuckled. "Nic's best friend. She's sort of psychic."

Ethan snorted and shook his head. "Bull. You know how I feel about woo-woo stuff. And people who claim to practice it."

"Aislinn doesn't claim to practice anything," Nic piped up in instant defensiveness on her friend's behalf. "She firmly denies having any psychic abilities at all. She's just very intuitive and gets uneasy feelings that come true sometimes. Lots of people have that ability."

Ethan still looked skeptical and fully prepared to argue about the existence—or lack thereof—of any sort of precognition, but Joel spoke quickly, as if to defuse any further argument. "So what have you two been talking about in here while I was in the other room?"

Nic and Ethan exchanged a look. "Just stuff," Nic said after a moment.

Joel frowned suspiciously, but Ethan made a smooth change of subject by mentioning the recent illness of an old acquaintance, which had the result of diverting Joel's attention. Nic filed her thoughts and questions about Joel's brother to the back of her mind during the remaining few minutes of their visit.

The dynamics of Joel's family were really none of her business, she reminded herself again—despite whatever private observations she might make during the rest of this informative weekend visit.

* * *

Because there was nothing left to do in Danston, Joel took Nic back to his parents' house when they left Ethan's place. He needed to spend more time with his folks anyway, he figured. His mom would be hurt if he didn't pay her enough attention during his visit.

He groaned softly when he saw the big black sedan parked in his parents' driveway. "Oh, great. I should have expected this."

"Someone you don't want to see?" Nic asked, following his line of vision.

He grimaced. "Wouldn't have been my first choice, no."

"Who is it?"

"My mother's best friend. Polly Albright."

"You don't like her?"

"I wouldn't want to say that, exactly," he hedged. "She has a good heart. And she's been a very good friend to my mother."

"But…?"

He sighed. "You'll just have to wait and see for yourself, I guess. But brace yourself for an inquisition. Polly has no sense of boundaries when it comes to finding out what she wants to know."

"That seems to be fairly common around here," Nic murmured.

He shrugged as he guided the car into one of the two garage bays. "It's pretty common in any town, isn't it? You know there are more than a few die-hard gossips back home."

"True. I guess I'm just not accustomed to being the focus of their attention. They generally consider me too boring to talk about."

"Yeah, well, they know you too well there," he teased lightly, turning off the engine. "Here you're fresh meat."

"Lovely." She reached for her door handle.

She'd been acting just a little oddly since they'd left Ethan's house, Joel mused as he climbed out of the car. Distracted. Thoughtful.

He couldn't help wondering what Ethan had said to her while he had been tied up on the phone. Neither Nic nor Ethan had seemed angry or sullen, but he'd gotten the sense that something had been said that had made both of them uncomfortable.

Unlike Polly, he wouldn't pry to try to find out what Nic and Ethan had talked about. But he had a sneaking suspicion it had been about him.

His mother and her guest were exactly where he expected to find them—sitting at the kitchen table drinking coffee, eating chocolates and chattering like magpies. They both looked around when he and Nic entered from the garage. The almost hungry expression on Polly's face reminded Joel a bit too vividly of his comment about Nic being "fresh meat."

"Joel." Polly braced her hands on the table to help hoist her sizable girth out of the chair.

As broad as she was tall, at just over five feet, Polly had never let her size slow her down. She was active in half a dozen local organizations, still worked a couple of days a week in the local elementary school office and had raised four children and an orphaned nephew. Her heart was big, and her fascination with other people's lives insatiable. Life was one long reality show to her, and much more interesting than the ones she watched religiously on television.

Because he really was fond of her despite her flaws, Joel smiled and leaned over to brush a kiss across her soft, puffy cheek. "Hello, Polly. You look as beautiful as ever. Don't you ever age?"

She giggled like a schoolgirl and playfully slapped his arm. "Full of blarney as always, I see. How are you holding up, hon?"

Her voice had gone from teasing to meltingly sympathetic within the space of those two sentences. Because he was all too accustomed to that transition during his visits here, he was able to handle it with a simple nod. "I'm fine, Polly. Thanks."

He turned immediately to Nic, drawing her forward with a motion of his hand. "Polly, I'd like you to meet a good friend of mine, Nicole Sawyer. Nic, this is Polly Albright, a dear friend of our family."

"It's very nice to meet you, Mrs. Albright."

Her avid eyes focused intently on Nic's face, Polly smiled. "Just call me Polly, hon. And it's real nice to meet you. Elaine's been telling me all about you."

Nic shot a quick glance at Joel's mother as if wondering what exactly had been said about her, but her smile didn't falter.

Polly motioned toward a chair. "Sit down, sweetie, and let's get to know each other. It's always such a pleasure to meet Joel's young friends."

To give her credit, Nic didn't let the consternation she must be feeling show in her eyes. Instead she accepted a cup of coffee from Elaine and took one of the empty seats at the kitchen table.

Joel was about to follow suit when Polly shook her head. "Go visit with your daddy, hon. I'm sure he'd like to spend time with you while you're here. Nicky will be fine here with us girls, won't you, dear?"

He happened to know she hated being called Nicky. And he was quite sure she would rather endure a root canal than sit in here with his mother and Polly for coffee and an inquisition. He couldn't quite meet her eyes as he did the only thing any man with a sense of self-preservation would do. He escaped, leaving Nic to fend for herself.

She had told him he would owe her for accompanying him on this trip at all. He didn't even want to think about how much he had just added to his tab.

Nic had just finished dressing for the party later that afternoon when her cell phone rang again. She sensed that it was Aislinn even before she checked the caller ID. Maybe she had a little psychic in her herself, she thought with a weak smile.

"I'm still okay," she said by way of answering. "Nothing bad has happened to me."

"I'm glad to hear that." But Aislinn didn't sound overly relieved. Her voice still held a note of concern. "I don't know why I keep worrying about you," she added somewhat sheepishly. "You know that isn't like me."

"No. It really isn't." Nic couldn't imagine what was setting Aislinn off like this. Aislinn wasn't prone to worrying, and Nic was hardly in a dangerous situation here, as she occasionally was on the job. Even then, Aislinn had expressed confidence in Nic's ability to take care of herself.

She could imagine all too well how Joel's fiercely pragmatic older brother would react to Aislinn's uncharacteristic attack of apprehension.

"Maybe you're just picking up my intense discomfort at being here at all," she suggested lightly. "But the only real danger is that I'm finally going to snap and do something that will really give these people something to gossip about."

Aislinn laughed a little at that. "Like what?"

"Oh, I don't know. Streak naked through the streets maybe? Get blitzed and dance on the tables at the party we're going to tonight?"

"I would so love to see you dancing on a table. But I don't think that has anything to do with my uneasy feelings."

"Then try not to worry anymore, okay? I'm really fine."

After a momentary pause, Aislinn asked, "It's really that bad?"

Nic tried to be honest. "Everyone is being very nice to me," she conceded. "Almost excessively so, at times. They're inquisitive. Some more than others—"

She almost shuddered as she remembered the awkward conversation with unabashedly nosy Polly

Albright. It had taken every bit of tact and patience Nic possessed—neither of which were characteristic traits—to get through that ordeal without actually resorting to rudeness.

"But it's been okay," she said. "And it's almost over now anyway."

"What about Joel's family? Are they being nice?"

"Yes." Though she thought Elaine could have done a little more to discourage Polly's prying. She suspected that Elaine had wanted to hear the answers herself but hadn't wanted to be the one to ask. "His father is quite charming. His mother's very gracious, though a little reserved—as if she isn't quite sure what I'm doing here. His brother—"

"His brother?" Aislinn prodded after a moment.

How could she describe Ethan? "I'll tell you more about him when I get back home," she promised.

"Sounds interesting."

"He is that."

"So you're going to a party tonight?"

"Yeah, and I'd better finish getting ready. Joel's going to want to leave soon."

"Then I won't hold you. Have a good time, Nic—and watch your back, okay? Just in case."

"I will. Thanks for caring."

Aislinn disconnected without saying goodbye.

Thoughtfully, Nic closed her phone and slipped it back into her purse before turning toward the mirror to make sure she was completely ready for the evening. Not having a clue what to wear for this event, she had settled for a go-anywhere black pantsuit.

A snug tunic-style jacket hugged what few curves she had and fell to just below her hips. Straight-legged lined pants fell softly to the top of her feet, on which she wore kitten-heeled mules with jet beadwork over the instep. Thin-wired chandelier earrings with red and black beads added a touch of color, along with a matching choker necklace. Surely no one could say she was wearing the wrong colors this time, she thought in satisfaction.

She had worn a little more makeup than usual—smoky gray shadow, subtle eyeliner, shimmering lip gloss. There wasn't much to do with her collar-length, layered honey hair, but she had washed it and blown it to a glossy shine.

Deciding she was as ready as she was ever going to be, she opened her bedroom door to find Joel standing on the other side, one hand raised as if to knock. They both laughed, but their amusement quickly faded as they gazed at each other.

"You look…great," Joel said, studying her almost as if he hadn't seen her in a long time.

"You clean up pretty well yourself," she replied. He really did look fantastic in his dark suit with a silvery-toned shirt and tie. Maybe he still wouldn't be mistaken for a movie heartthrob, but he definitely had an attraction of his own.

She actually found him a little too appealing for her own peace of mind at that moment. She was suddenly having all these crazy thoughts about running her hands beneath that conservative jacket to feel the muscles she knew it concealed. Wondering how it might feel to be cradled against that solid chest and have that nicely shaped mouth pressed against hers.

"Ready to go?" he asked after a moment, and his voice sounded a little strained, as if he had somehow guessed the direction her wayward thoughts had taken.

She nodded and tucked her purse beneath her arm.

She was beginning to wonder if Aislinn was right about her being in danger here after all. Not a physical threat, which Nic knew how to deal with, but a risk to her heart.

That was one part of herself that she had never actually put into harm's way before—and she didn't want to change that record now, especially with a man who couldn't be more wrong for her. At least that was the opinion of his family and friends—and surely they knew him better than she did.

Glittering in sequins, Heidi met people at the door of the ballroom as they arrived for the party. Armed with a beaming smile and stick-on name tags, she ushered them inside and urged everyone to have a "fabulous" time.

"Nicole," she semisquealed when Nic and Joel entered. "I'm so glad you're here. There's someone you absolutely have to meet."

"Oh? Who's that?'

"His name is Jimmy Waller. You remember Jimmy, don't you, Joel?"

"Of course. He sat beside me in half my classes. I don't think I've seen him since graduation."

"That's because he went into the Navy. He's been overseas every time we've had a reunion before. He just retired from the military last month, and you'll never guess what he's doing now."

"No, I—"

"He's a police officer," Heidi cut in with an arch look at Nic. "He lives in Memphis, Tennessee—not too far from where you two live, is it?"

"No, not far." Joel sounded oddly grudging as he made the admission.

"Isn't that nice? And the best part is he's single and he's even cuter than he was in high school. You and Jimmy should have a lot to talk about, Nicole."

Nic felt her eyes go wide. Was Heidi actually trying to set her up? Even though she was here as Joel's, if not date, at least companion? "I, uh—"

Joel surprised her by wrapping an arm loosely around her shoulders and telling Heidi warmly, "We'll both enjoy talking to him. I'd love the chance to catch up with Jimmy."

Nic couldn't quite describe his attitude. Not possessive exactly. After all, why would he be feeling at all possessive? The arm around the shoulders could be taken for a friendly, just-pals sort of gesture—even though she felt her nerve endings tingling all along the path of contact. But that was her issue, not Joel's. He was probably just trying to keep her from feeling embarrassed by Heidi's blatant matchmaking.

Heidi's gaze lingered for several moments on

Joel's arm, but her smile didn't fade as she handed them each a name tag and waved them inside. "Go find Jimmy. I'm sure he'll be delighted to see you both."

Chapter Eight

"I can't imagine why Heidi thought we needed these," Joel muttered, glancing down at the gold-bordered white paper tag on his lapel. "We all know each other. And I really don't need the doctor title in front of my name for a gathering with old friends. It looks so pretentious."

"No one who knows you would ever call you pretentious," Nic assured him. "Everyone knows this was Heidi's idea."

As foolish as it made her feel, she stuck her own tag somewhat crookedly on her chest. Fortunately Heidi hadn't felt it necessary to add *Officer* to Nic's name. Maybe they'd been printed before she had learned that tidbit.

The Watson twins were in attendance, of course, both looking uncomfortable in suits and ties their wives had undoubtedly made them wear. A few other people Nic had met the night before greeted them, and she made the requisite small talk as they worked their way across the room.

She was relieved to see that her black pantsuit fit in perfectly. The other women had dressed in a range from Sunday best to shimmering cocktail outfits, and hers fell nicely in between.

She found it both amusing and a little sad that Heidi had chosen to decorate as if they were attending a high school party. Red, white and silver balloons and streamers seemed to be multiplying in every corner. Glittery banners proclaimed, Always Cardinals, Always Friends. Joel informed her that it had been the theme of their senior prom.

The brand-new second-story ballroom wasn't huge but large enough to easily accommodate the group. The floor was gleaming wood, suitable for dancing, and a wall of glass doors gave a view of the wood-railed lanai built invitingly over a sloping drop down to the lake. Because it was such a mild evening, the doors were open, and several people were out on the lighted lanai admiring the moonlight reflecting on the water below.

Large posters decorated with pictures from their school days were displayed on easels arranged around the ballroom. Nic spent some time studying them, diverted by the images of the younger Watson brothers and some of the other balding or burgeoning classmates.

It was inevitable that a disproportionate number of the pictures were of Joel and Heather, separately and together. After all, they had been leaders in their class, popular, attractive and apparently active in every school activity.

Nic wondered idly how many photos of her a committee could find for a class reunion. She hadn't been much of a "joiner," and her activities had generally been outside of school. Community softball and soccer teams, martial arts studio in a nearby town, the rest of her free time spent mostly with her family. Her classmates would remember her, of course, but certainly not with the intense admiration—bordering on near reverence—that this group showed for Heather.

Tables had been arranged around the perimeter of the large ballroom, each seating eight people. A buffet table with covered serving dishes sat against one wall, uniformed servers waiting behind them. The center of the room had been left clear, presumably to serve as a dance floor.

Nic didn't see a band but spotted some equipment in a secluded nook that indicated a DJ would probably show up later. If she had one, she would call her bookie to bet that the music would be exactly the same playlist from that long-ago senior prom.

Joel led her to a table where two couples were already seated. She didn't remember any of these people from the night before, and the greetings they exchanged with Joel told her she was right in guessing they hadn't attended the game. Both couples were African-American, and their genuine pleasure at seeing Joel again reinforced her impression that he had been friends with all the different groups and cliques in his class.

"It's great to see everyone," Joel said after shaking hands with the men and exchanging air kisses with the women. "I was hoping you'd show up."

"We were sorry to miss the game last night," one of the men said. "Terrell and I both had to work yesterday and didn't get off in time to get here for the game. We drove in together this morning."

"You all still live in Birmingham?"

All four smiled and nodded.

Joel drew her forward. "This is my friend, Nicole Sawyer. Nic, I'd like you to meet Kevin Bender and his wife, Naomi. And this is Kevin's cousin, Terrell Bender, and his wife, Latricia. Kevin, Naomi and Terrell were all in my class, and I met Latricia at the last reunion."

Nic smiled and nodded to each in turn. She was impressed that Joel remembered everyone's name—but maybe he was just really quick and subtle at reading name tags. "It's nice to meet you."

"Heidi said we'll be eating soon, and Terrell and I are way past ready," Kevin confided. "Lunch was a long time ago. Y'all want to sit here to eat with us?"

"We'd love to join you," Joel accepted quickly, pulling out a chair and motioning for Nic to be seated.

Something about his manner made her wonder if he was deliberately avoiding being seated with the Watson twins again, who had two extra places at their nearby table and were looking their way. Maybe he'd had enough of them the night before. Or maybe he just wanted to visit with some other old friends for a while and had no ulterior motives at all.

They went through the usual ceremony of looking at children's photos, catching up on job advances and extended family news. It didn't take Nic long to figure out that she was sitting among a group of successful professionals. She learned that Terrell was a professor of mathematics and that his attractive wife Latricia was a cohost on a morning television news-and-features program. Kevin was an architect, and Naomi an elementary school principal. They all expressed interest in Nic's career, but it was obvious that they were surprised by her occupation.

"Is everybody getting hungry?" Heidi chirped, approaching their table with a pleasantly plain-featured man in tow. "We're about to open the buffet lines."

Terrell assured her earnestly that he was about ready to start chewing on the red-and-white-flower centerpiece.

Heidi laughed, then waved the man with her to one of the two empty chairs. The one next to Nic. "I'm sure you all remember Jimmy. You don't mind if he joins you for dinner, do you? Nic, this is the man I was telling you about. Officer Jimmy Waller, this is Joel's pal, Officer Nicole Sawyer. I bet the two of you have lots of exciting police stuff to talk about."

With that, she was gone, bustling over to the buffet table to direct the servers as the dishes were uncovered and tantalizing aromas filled the room.

Having spoken to his old classmates and been introduced to Latricia, Jimmy turned to Nic with a rueful smile in his friendly brown eyes. "So, Nicole, do you have any 'exciting police stuff' to talk about?"

She laughed. "I'm afraid not. You're the one from the big-city PD. Maybe you'd like to try to impress everyone with tales of your adventures."

Grinning, he shook his head. "Actually, I'd rather eat. We'd better head over that way before the Watson twins clean out the serving dishes."

"Good suggestion," Kevin said, jumping to his feet. "From what I remember, those boys can really put away the food."

Joel held Nic back a few steps as the others rushed toward the growing food line. "Sorry again about Heidi," he said. "Don't feel like you have to personally entertain Jimmy just because he's a cop and he came stag tonight."

"No problem. He seems very nice."

"Well, he was a nice enough guy back in school," Joel agreed guardedly. "But I haven't seen him in fifteen years, and people can change, you know."

Was he actually warning her off Jimmy? He wasn't motivated by jealousy, of course, but maybe he didn't want her attention to be too far distracted from her purpose in being there—serving as a buffer between Joel and the sympathy of his classmates.

She thought it best not to tell him that he didn't have to worry about her paying too little attention to him. The unsettling truth was, she was having trouble focusing on anyone else but him this weekend.

Joel couldn't say he was enjoying the party, exactly. It was great to see Kevin and Terrell again, but after the first hour they had pretty well caught up. By the time they finished their entrées and were making their way through desserts, they were having trouble coming up with anything new to talk about. Nic and Jimmy, however, seemed to be having no such difficulty.

Maybe it was because they were both cops. Gave them something in common to discuss. Stories to swap, bad guys to compare.

Just because they were laughing a lot and seemed to be enjoying their conversation certainly didn't mean they were flirting. Exactly. Or that they were making a connection that might go somewhere after this evening ended. It was just dinner conversation—and none of his business anyway.

He didn't like it. And because that disapproval made him feel petty and selfish, he brooded even more, though he did his best to hide it.

The buffet tables were covered and rolled away and a hired DJ took his place behind his equipment, signaling that the dinner portion of the party was over and the dance part was about to begin. Joel glanced at his watch, wondering how soon he and Nic could politely make their escape. If he could drag her away from her new best pal, he thought with a scowl.

Kevin and Naomi were among the first couples on the dance floor. Terrell and Latricia had wandered off to talk to some other couples, leaving Joel, Nic and Jimmy at the table, where Nic and Jimmy were engaged in a discussion about recent legislation concerning high-speed chases.

The way Nic was looking so intently at Jimmy made Joel frown and then rise abruptly to his feet. "Come on, Nic. Let's dance."

It was hardly the most gracious invitation he had ever extended. Nic's look of surprise let him know that she hadn't been expecting him to ask. Had she not planned to dance this evening? Or had it not even crossed her mind that he might want to dance with her?

"Okay," she said, standing. "Sure. Excuse us, please, Jimmy."

"You bet. Maybe I can steal a dance later?"

She smiled. "I think that can be arranged."

Joel could feel his eyebrows sinking into a deeper frown even as he drew Nic into a loose hold on the dance floor. After swaying for a moment in silence, she tipped her head back to look up at him. "What's wrong, Joel? Is something bothering you?"

He made a deliberate effort to smooth his expression. "No, I'm okay. Just getting a little tired of the reunion thing. How about you? Are you having a good time?"

"Surprisingly, yes. Your friends are all very nice, aren't they?"

Was she talking about all his old friends—or one in particular? "Yeah, most of them are really great."

"The food was even good, which is always surprising at a function like this. One thing about Heidi—she knows how to put on a party."

"She lives for that sort of thing." He was peripherally aware that they were being watched from various places around the room with varying degrees of curiosity and contemplation, but that didn't seem to matter at the moment. What did matter was the surprisingly natural feel of Nic in his arms, the easy way she matched her steps to his. It didn't feel like a first dance but as if they had been dancing together for a long time.

It felt nice. Better than nice, actually.

He'd known Nic was in excellent physical condition, her compact body toned and strong. But it was different observing something about her and actually feeling it with his own hands. Her warmth radiated through the silky fabric of her clothing, and her soft hair brushed his chin when she turned her head to smile at someone else on the floor.

She seemed different tonight somehow. Softer. Smaller. He was still fully aware of her self-sufficiency, her competence, the fiery temper that had been known to make lawbreakers recoil. All things he admired in his friend and his neighbor. But tonight he was also seeing her through fresh eyes. And what he saw was a very attractive young woman with a great body and an infectious smile.

It occurred to him only then that he had been seeing her that way for longer than he'd been willing to admit.

She was looking at him oddly then, as if his

behavior was beginning to puzzle her. He forced a smile and said the first thing that popped into his mind. "You're a good dancer."

"Thanks. I like to dance. I always wanted to take ballroom lessons, but I've just never found the time. Maybe someday."

He and Heather had taken ballroom dance lessons one summer when they'd both been home from college. They had always planned to take more eventually. "Not a lot of places to dance back home," he said.

"Certainly not ballroom dancing. Brad and I used to dance at the Boot-Scoot Barn sometimes. Line dancing and western swing mostly."

The mention of her ex almost made him scowl again, but he managed to keep his expression bland. He didn't know why he was so grumpy this evening.

"You and Jimmy seem to be hitting it off," he said, the words popping out before he'd planned to say them. "Heidi must be pleased."

Nic wrinkled her nose. "We have our jobs in common. That's the only reason I can think of that Heidi was so intent on introducing us."

"Maybe she was doing a little matchmaking. Since you and I have made it so clear we're only friends, I suppose she thought she was doing you a favor."

Nic shrugged, the movement bringing her more closely against him—and almost derailing his entire train of thought. "He's a nice guy and all but not really my type. For one thing, I'd never want to get involved with another cop—and I bet Jimmy feels the same way."

"So what *is* your type?" he asked in a murmur. "Cowboys?"

She chuckled. "We both know that didn't work out. Maybe I just don't have a type."

"Or maybe you just haven't realized yet what you're looking for."

Laughter lit her face. "Or maybe I'm just not looking," she quipped.

His gaze focused on her smiling lips, and he couldn't resist smiling back at her. His mood was suddenly much lighter—and he knew exactly why.

Just to amuse her, he raised his arm to spin her, then finished the dance with a shallow dip. The ploy worked nicely; she laughed and clung to his forearms for balance. And when he steadied her on her feet again, he couldn't resist brushing a light kiss against her cheek.

"Thanks for the dance," he said, wondering if his voice sounded as odd to her as it suddenly did to him. "It was fun."

Her cheeks were flushed now, but he wasn't sure if the heightened color was due to the kiss or the mild exertion of the dance. "You're welcome," she said.

There were a few more dances, some with each other, some with other partners. Joel didn't even mind—that much—when she finally danced with Jimmy. He danced with Naomi that time, only glancing Nic's way once or twice, each time concluding that she had been honest in saying she wasn't particularly attracted to his onetime classmate. At least that was what he wanted to believe, and he didn't take time to ask himself why it mattered so much.

After an hour or so of dancing, Heidi borrowed the DJ's mic to draw everyone's attention her way. Traditionally the class president would have emceed the occasion, but Joel had declined that privilege, asking Heidi to take over his duties. He hadn't had to twist her arm to persuade her to accept.

Her sequined top glittering in the overhead lights, Heidi beamed with pleasure at being the center of attention. She looked pleased with the results of her months of planning, and as he and everyone else returned to their tables, Joel felt a bit guilty for not appreciating her efforts more.

"I hope you all enjoyed the food tonight," she began, and was answered by nods and smiles from her audience. "We want to thank Big Daddy's Catering for their excellent service. And a special thanks to our DJ, Chico Morales." An enthusiastic round of applause followed.

"Before we continue our dance, I'd like to take care of a little business. First, thank you all for coming and making our fifteen-year reunion such a great success. Starting with our victory in last night's game," she added—for all the world, Joel thought, as if their class had been out on the field catching passes.

Hoots and cheers sounded through the room, most loudly from the Watson twins, who seemed to have brought their own liquid refreshments for the party. And they weren't the only ones.

"Also," Heidi continued when the noise died down, "I want to remind everyone to sign the big get-well card for our beloved Principal Walenski. We hope he recovers quickly from his recent illness. And now to our awards…"

Joel couldn't quite suppress a low groan, a sound that was echoed by Kevin and Terrell.

Nic looked questioningly at him. "Awards?"

He shook his head. "You'll see."

Giggling like the schoolgirl she still wanted to be, Heidi read from a sheet of paper. "First, the classmate with the most children…Janie Caruthers Mayo, mother of five! The newest only ten weeks old."

Amid hearty applause, Heidi presented the blushing mother with a large bottle of over-the-counter headache pills, a box of condoms and a gift certificate for a dinner out at a local restaurant.

"Oh," Nic murmured. "That kind of award."

Joel nodded. "She does this every time. She still thinks it's hysterically funny."

"Awards" and silly gifts were then presented for the classmate who had traveled farthest to attend the reunion, to one who had recently been elected mayor of a neighboring small town and to another who had recently retired after a moderately successful career in professional baseball. The latter was treated to a box containing denture adhesives, a knitted lap scarf and a book of crossword puzzles, among other supposedly humorous references to retirement. Joel noted that Donald didn't look overly amused, though he made an effort to smile appreciatively.

Heidi then read a few notes from former classmates who hadn't been able to attend the reunion but had sent greetings. When the laughter over the final, particularly cleverly worded message faded away, Heidi cleared her throat and spoke more seriously. "Finally I would like to announce the kickoff of our new charitable project. It's getting off to an amazing start, with almost eight thousand dollars donated so far...."

Joel frowned. He couldn't remember being notified of a new charity project. He was quite sure he hadn't been asked to donate to it, though of course he would be happy to contribute. He made a mental note to do so immediately after...

He was startled to hear Heidi say his name into the microphone. "Joel, would you join me here for just a minute, please?"

Chapter Nine

Something about the way his tablemates looked at him when Heidi called his name made Joel suspect that all of them except Nic knew what was coming next. Nic looked as curious as he felt about why he had been summoned forward.

Trying to hide his reluctance behind a smile, he stood and crossed the room to join Heidi. "What is this?"

Her blue eyes suddenly liquid, Heidi's answering smile quivered a bit as she gazed up at him. "The rest of us have put together a surprise for you, Joel. Tonight it is my honor and my pleasure to announce that our class has established the Heather Shields Brannon Scholarship Fund, to be awarded annually to two deserving Danston High School graduates, to be used for furthering their educations."

Joel felt his embarrassment and mild irritation dissolve immediately. He was immeasurably touched by his classmates' gesture. "Heidi, this is…"

Her smile growing steadier, she shook her head. "Not just me. All of us. Everyone donated."

She pressed the microphone into his hand and stepped back, making it clear that he was expected to say something. He hoped he would be able to find the words.

"This is incredible," he began, looking out at the smiling faces surrounding him. "I can't think of any memorial that would please Heather more than a scholarship in her name. She loved Danston High, and nothing would make her happier than to know that a new generation of students will benefit from her having attended there. Heather loved all of you, too. On her behalf, I would like to thank you for keeping her memory and her spirit alive in our school and in your hearts."

Oh, man, had that been too sappy? He'd meant every word, but he hoped they hadn't sounded glib or trite. When his classmates rose to their feet to applaud, he swallowed hard, handed the microphone back to Heidi and hurried back to his table, wondering if anyone would notice if he just kept walking right out the door.

Even as she stood and applauded along with everyone else in the room, Nic felt as though her smile was frozen on her face. She couldn't have described how she was feeling at that moment. The scholarship was a nice gesture, of course, and she could tell that the announcement had affected Joel. Heck, she would probably donate to it herself before the weekend was over.

Joel's parents would probably be moved to tears when he told them about it. Ethan wouldn't show his emotions, but she suspected he would be as deeply affected as the others, especially if what she suspected about his feelings for his late sister-in-law was true.

It took Joel a while to make his way back to the table. People kept stopping him—the men to shake his hand and clap him on the shoulder, the women to hug him, many with tears streaming down their faces. To his credit, Joel kept his composure admirably, though Nic thought she could see the effort it was costing him.

This, she realized, was what he had been dreading all weekend. A tearful and sentimental tribute to his late wife. While he was obviously touched by their affection and their generosity, he was equally overwhelmed by the outpouring of emotions that brought back so many difficult memories for him.

Naomi reached out to hug him when he finally reached their table. His eyes met Nic's over Naomi's head, and she could see that he was quickly reaching his breaking point.

Fortunately the DJ had returned to his duties, deliberately brightening the mood of the party with a peppy oldie that drew a few couples irresistibly back

NO POSTAGE
NECESSARY
IF MAILED
IN THE
UNITED STATES

BUSINESS REPLY MAIL
FIRST-CLASS MAIL   PERMIT NO. 717-003   BUFFALO, NY

POSTAGE WILL BE PAID BY ADDRESSEE

SILHOUETTE READER SERVICE
3010 WALDEN AVE
PO BOX 1867
BUFFALO NY 14240-9952

onto the dance floor. The moment Naomi released Joel, Nic stepped forward to grab his hand.

"I think we need one more dance before we head back to your parents' house, don't you?" she asked brightly.

His fingers closed around hers so tightly that she had to suppress a wince. "Yes, I think we do," he agreed too heartily and all but towed her onto the dance floor.

It wasn't a particularly slow number, but he drew her into his arms anyway, matching their steps to the tempo without releasing her. Nic wondered if he just needed to hold on to someone for a few minutes, a form of physical and emotional support.

"Thank you," he said after a moment. "I needed this."

"It really was a nice thing for them to have done, Joel."

"I know. I can't get over how great it was of them. They managed to take me completely by surprise. I had no idea they were planning anything like this."

"A scholarship fund is such a perfect tribute. Much better than a memorial plaque or something static like that."

"Exactly. I hope the kids who benefit from it will really make the school proud. I just wish—"

"You wish they hadn't sprung it on you in front of everyone so that you had no private time to absorb it and decide what to say in response."

"That's exactly what I wish," he admitted, seemingly grateful that she understood. "I don't want to sound at all ungrateful, but it would have been nice if they'd told me what they were doing and had given me a chance to prepare a little speech beforehand."

"I get the impression Heidi loves surprises. I bet she's inflicted surprise birthday parties on everyone she knows."

"As a matter of fact, she even got my dad once. And he hates surprise parties."

She could feel the muscles in his arms and shoulders starting to relax. He'd been so tense when they had started the dance. She was glad her matter-of-fact tone seemed to be setting him more at ease. "I wonder if Heidi told your father about the scholarship."

"I doubt it. She wouldn't trust him to keep quiet about it. I'll tell my family about it."

"They'll be pleased."

His head very close to hers, he nodded. "Yes, they will."

She was even more aware than before that others were watching them as they danced. She supposed his classmates wondered how she felt about the tribute to her escort's late wife. As hard as they had tried, she wasn't sure she and Joel had been entirely successful in convincing everyone that there was nothing but friendship between them. Or maybe they believed Joel thought of it that way but that she was hoping for more.

That made sense, in a way. There were several single women in Joel's class, and more than one had eyed him in a way that made her suspect they had hoped he would come alone to the reunion. They would probably stand in line to offer him comfort and companionship in the loneliness they projected onto him.

If Heidi were any indication, Joel's friends couldn't see her taking Heather's place in his life. Or in theirs.

As she had so many times during the past couple of days, she wondered if it was something in particular about her that bothered them. Or would they have been as reluctant to see any other woman try to step into Saint Heather's shoes?

"I think we've done our share of socializing tonight, don't you?" Joel asked with a quick glance around the room that let her know he was as aware of their audience as she was. "I think we can politely leave after this dance."

While the event hadn't been as dull or as awkward as she had feared, it was with great relief that Nic seized on his offer of escape. "Absolutely. Other people are already leaving. It won't look at all odd if we call it a night."

He seemed pleased that she had agreed. When the music ended, he turned with her toward their table, keeping a hand lightly at the small of her back as they moved across the clearing dance floor.

They said their good-nights quickly, promising to see most of his friends the next morning at the farewell breakfast. Without giving Heidi a chance to detain them, they slipped out, barely escaping the Watson twins, who had been weaving in their direction.

* * *

Nic noticed that Joel didn't turn in the direction of his parents' house when he left the resort, but she didn't comment. Maybe he just needed to take the scenic route and unwind a little before he went back. She suspected he wasn't really looking forward to telling his parents about the scholarship, probably expecting an overly emotional response from his mother.

The car radio was turned off, and it was very quiet within his father's big sedan. The silence was actually nice for a little while, in contrast to the noise of the party, but eventually Nic felt the urge to say something. She glanced his way, studying his profile in the shadows of the car. The dim green lights from the dashboard did little to reveal his expression to her. "Did you have a good time tonight?"

"For the most part. What did Jimmy give you when we were leaving?"

She hadn't thought he'd noticed the quick exchange. Not that she was trying to hide anything from him, of course, but she hadn't wanted to make a big deal of it. "He gave me his home number. You know, just in case anything ever comes up when I might need a professional contact in Memphis."

"And why would you need that?"

"I don't know," she admitted with a shrug. "But it could happen."

"He was hitting on you."

She sighed. "He wasn't hitting on me. It was just a professional courtesy."

"You exchange phone numbers with every cop you meet?"

"Well, no, but…"

"He was hitting on you."

Her sigh was louder this time. "He was not hitting on me."

Joel didn't respond that time, but something about his silence made his skepticism clear.

Shaking her head, Nic looked out the window. He was driving along the lake road, and the water looked beautiful with the half-moon reflected across it. On the other side of the lake lay the resort they'd just left. Lights burned in multiple windows, but they were too far away now to tell how many people were still moving around inside the ballroom.

Joel turned onto a side road marked by a sign that pointed out a boat launch area ahead. The gravel road wound through a stand of trees, which made it all the darker inside the quiet car. Joel followed the road to an empty parking lot beside the launch ramp and drove into a parking space facing the lake. Without a word, he turned off the headlights and then the engine, leaving them in darkness and silence.

Had he been anyone else, she might have thought he'd brought her to this secluded, scenic spot for a quick grab-and-grope session. As it was, she figured he was just stalling before going back to his parents' house.

She could be a good friend now, let him talk about his feelings, give him a bracing pat on the back, if necessary. And she wouldn't be at all disappointed about the lack of grabbing and groping during that talk, she vowed.

She gave him time to begin the conversation in his own way. Braced for Heather's name, she was dumbfounded when he said, "Jimmy's a pretty nice guy, but I've heard rumors that he's been married twice."

"We're still talking about Jimmy?" She shook her head in bemusement. "Why?"

"Just thought you should know."

"Joel, I keep telling you there's nothing between Jimmy and me. Why on earth do you keep obsessing about him?"

He turned then, and his face was barely discernible in the deep shadows lightened only by the pale moonlight. "I don't know," he admitted after a minute. "First it was Heidi trying to fix you up. And then you and Jimmy got along so well. And then he gave you his number…."

"He was just being friendly. We had a few things in common—we're both cops and we were the only two people at the table without advanced degrees—but that was the extent of it. I doubt that I'll ever hear from him again. But even if he was hitting on me—which he wasn't—I'm a big girl, Joel. I can tell a guy no if I'm not interested. And I can say yes when I am without needing any brotherly warnings or advice."

"Brotherly?" He sounded thoughtful as he repeated the word. "You think I'm being brotherly?"

"Well, maybe buddy-ly," she said with a chuckle

at her own bad joke. "But it isn't necessary, Joel. I'm perfectly capable of—"

"Of knowing when someone's interested in you?" he cut in. "Of being aware when a man wants more from you than friendship?"

Had he been anyone else, she thought with a ripple of doubt, she might have read too much into those questions. "Well, yeah."

"Then it shouldn't surprise you," he said, reaching toward her, "if I do this."

He was wrong, she thought even as his mouth covered hers. She was more than surprised by this totally unexpected kiss. She was flabbergasted.

It seemed like a long time before Joel lifted his head, though the kiss probably lasted only a few moments. His mouth only an inch or so above hers, he searched her face in the very little light that was available to him.

She was glad it was dark. She didn't want him seeing her expression too clearly at that moment, since she wasn't at all sure what it would reveal to him.

"Well?" he asked after a moment. "Are you still so sure you always know when a man wants you?"

"But you...we...we're not..." Annoyed with herself for stammering, she stopped and drew a deep breath before trying again. "You and I are just friends."

"I know. At least that's what I've tried to be to you," he added. "But lately...I don't know. Something's changed."

This was absolutely the very last thing she had expected this evening. Especially now, after that big tribute to Heather.

He drew back a little farther, not quite releasing her but giving her more space. "Look, if you're not interested, it's okay. I don't regret giving it a shot, but I can go back to the way things were before if that's what you want. We'll never mention any of this again."

Her head spinning a little, Nic tried to decide exactly how she felt. "It isn't that I'm not interested," she said finally. "I just— Well, I'm not so sure it's a good idea. I mean, you're one of my best friends, you know? I wouldn't want to do anything to mess that up."

"Neither would I."

Nodding, she added, "Besides, I'm a little concerned about the timing of this thing. You know, here in your hometown during your reunion, when your emotions are all stirred up and confused. It would probably be best if we didn't start anything here that we might both regret later."

He took his hands away from her then, settling back into his own seat. "You're suggesting that I don't know what I'm doing?"

Oops. Definitely a hint of wounded male ego there. Funny. She'd never seen evidence of it in Joel before—but then, he'd never made a pass at her before, either. As badly as she was handling this, he probably never would again.

That realization left her feeling oddly depressed—and wondering what she could say to keep from closing that door altogether. "I didn't say you don't know what you're doing. I just wonder if you would have ever said these things to me if we hadn't come to your reunion."

"I think I would have…eventually. Even though I've been trying to deny it, the attraction has been there for a long time. I guess I was just waiting for the right time."

"And you thought that was tonight?" She knew she sounded skeptical, but it was hard to completely hide her doubts that he'd been able to conceal so completely the attraction he claimed to have felt. She didn't know what exactly had triggered his kissing her, but she found it hard to believe he'd been suffering from unrequited lust for her.

More likely he was just feeling a bit lost and lonely after the evening with his old friends, most of whom appeared to be happily paired off. He had needed to reach out, and she was the closest woman available.

It occurred to her that her conclusion wasn't particularly flattering to either of them, but that didn't change the possibility that she was right.

He reached for the car key. "I guess you've made it clear enough that I was wrong."

She reached out quickly and laid her hand on his arm before he could start the engine. "You've really been attracted to me?"

He went still for a moment, then replied in a wry voice, "Let's just say I had a hard time hiding how pleased I was when Cowboy Brad rode off into the sunset."

She swallowed hard. Was Joel actually implying that he had been jealous of Brad? "You hid it very well."

"Now you know."

Her hand still rested on his arm. She could feel the muscles bunched beneath her fingertips, an indication of the tension that gripped him. She was suddenly reminded of that moment outside the guest bedroom the night before, when their eyes had locked and something powerful had passed between them.

She'd convinced herself then that her imagination had gotten away from her. Now she was rethinking that assumption.

"Maybe…" She moistened her lips and tried again. "Maybe we could talk about this again. When we get back home. If you still want to, I mean."

He surprised her yet again by chuckling, though it was just a weary murmur of a sound. "Am I to take that to mean that you might be interested after all?"

"I never said I wasn't interested," she reminded him again. "But I think we need to take this very slowly and cautiously if we're going to try to change our relationship."

"Slow and cautious?" This time his amusement was a bit more pronounced. "That doesn't sound like the Nic Sawyer I know."

"Yes, well, that Nic Sawyer's been burned more than once. And this time there's a lot more to lose if something goes wrong," she added candidly. "I didn't mind so much when things fell apart with Cow—

with Brad. But if anything happened to ruin things between us…well, that would be hard for me to accept."

His expression completely hidden in the darkness, he reached again for the ignition key. "We'd better get back. It's getting late."

Wistfully acknowledging that the awkward discussion was at an end and wondering if she could have handled it better, she sat back in her seat and looked out the window as he backed the car out of the parking space. It was so pretty here, she thought, her gaze lingering on the rippling, moonlight-streaked water. He couldn't have chosen a more romantic spot to bring her to.

She couldn't help but wonder if this had been a place where he'd often brought Heather.

Though she and Lou had already turned in, Elaine had left a few lights on downstairs for Joel and Nic's sake. Joel turned them off behind them as he escorted Nic through the kitchen and up the stairs toward their bedrooms.

They reached her door first, and he paused there with her. "Good night, Nic. Sleep well."

As if that were going to happen now. She doubted that she would sleep a wink. But she said only, "Thanks. You, too."

She reached for the doorknob.

This time he was the one who reached out to stop her movement, his hand covering hers on the brass knob. The metal was cold beneath her palm, his skin very warm on the top of her hand. The contrast made a funny shiver run down her spine, and she swallowed hard before looking up at him in question. She didn't say anything because she didn't quite trust her voice to remain steady.

He held her eyes with his own. "What you said in the car—that you didn't want to do anything to mess up our friendship? I just want you to know that I feel exactly the same way."

"So you don't think we should—"

"What?" he asked when she hesitated. "Do this?"

He bent his head and kissed her. There was more confidence this time, more familiarity. Less tentative exploration and more heat. She wanted to grab him by the tie and drag him into the room behind her, letting them both find out exactly how much more they could have than platonic friendship.

It was a long time before he lifted his head, and when his eyes met hers again, she saw a similar sentiment mirrored there.

He lifted his hand to cup her cheek. "Nic, I—"

"Joel?" Elaine stood at the end of the hallway, just at the top of the stairs, looking their way with a frown. Neither of them had heard her approaching, and they both froze at the sound of her voice.

Joel dropped his hand, though he didn't immediately step away from Nic. "What do you need, Mom?"

"I was just making sure you got home okay. Um...do either of you need anything?"

"No, thank you, Mrs. Brannon. I'm fine," Nic

replied, proud that she'd managed to keep her voice steady despite her tumultuous emotions.

"We're good, Mom. Good night."

"Good night." But she didn't move, and Nic got the feeling she didn't intend to until Nic and Joel were safely closed into separate bedrooms.

To make it easier on all of them, Nic took the initiative. "G'night, Joel. I'll see you in the morning."

Without giving him a chance to respond, she stepped backward into the guest bedroom and shut the door.

Maybe Nic had questions about whether she and Joel should even try to go beyond friendship, but she knew Elaine had no doubts at all that it would be a horrible mistake.

Chapter Ten

Nic didn't usually wear much makeup for daytime, but she donned a bit more than usual Sunday morning in a vain effort to hide the shadows beneath her eyes. Sleep had been elusive, and the results of her restless tossing and turning were visible in her face. An extra dab of concealer and sweep of blush had little effect, she noted in discontent, studying her face in the mirror.

The vivid red sweater she wore with gray slacks and black boots was another attempt at optical illusion. The bright, cheery color—the one she should have worn to the football game, she thought ruefully—should draw attention away from her face. At least that was her intention.

Not that she expected it to fool Joel for a minute. The most she could hope was that he looked a bit ragged himself this morning.

If only they didn't have to attend this farewell breakfast. A few of the former classmates had mentioned that they were skipping this part at the party last night. Jimmy, for example, had said he would be leaving quite early this morning.

But Heidi had insisted on one last gathering to see everyone off, especially since so many were staying at the resort and would be wanting breakfast before they left anyway. Joel hadn't seemed to know how to bow out gracefully—a real weakness of his.

She could handle another hour or so, Nic promised herself. She could keep smiling and nodding and pretending there was nothing on her mind but socializing with Joel and his friends. And when she returned home, she would stay very busy with work, giving herself—and Joel—time to decide if they had been swept up in a moment, carried away by feelings that couldn't last.

Joel was dressed before Nic. He could hear her moving around in her room as he passed by, but he didn't stop to knock. She would come out when she was ready and she didn't need him to escort her downstairs.

He walked through his mother's hallway photo gallery, somberly studying the images as he passed them. He hadn't actually realized until now how many photos of Heather his mother had on display.

Nor had he given a thought to how a new woman in his life might feel about walking through this shrine to his late wife.

It hadn't been necessary to think along those lines before. Nic was the first woman he'd brought to his parents' home since Heather died.

Though he hadn't intended to, he paused in front of a huge framed photograph of himself and Heather on their wedding day. She had been so beautiful, and he had looked so happy. And though they had waited longer than some young couples to marry, preferring to finish their career training first, they had both looked so damned young.

Just over five years had passed since that photo was taken, but he felt so much older. So different. Maybe that was why he found himself falling now for a very different type of woman.

He had known Heather better than he'd ever known anyone, including his family. He had watched her grow from a giggly girl to a polished, professional woman. They had shared everything with each other, their dreams, their fears, their joys and disappointments. And yet he couldn't say with any certainty now how Heather would have felt about Nic. What she would think about his growing feelings for Nic.

Like most couples, they'd had a talk soon after they married in which they'd discussed the unlikely event that one of them would die an untimely death, leaving the other widowed at an early age. Smug in their confidence that nothing like that could ever happen to them, the golden couple of Danston High, they had earnestly made each other promise that they would never be lonely and miserable, no matter what.

"I would want you to fall in love again," Heather had assured him. "You're the type of man who thrives in a steady, supportive relationship. I would never want you to be alone."

"And I would want you to remarry," Joel had assured her in return, knowing even then that he was lying through his teeth.

Yeah, he'd wanted her to be happy—but he couldn't imagine her with anyone but him. Couldn't bear to think about it. Had Heather felt the same way despite her unselfish words?

"Joel?"

He hadn't heard Nic's door open. Hearing her voice right behind him made him turn away from the wedding portrait with a start that felt unjustifiably guilty. "Oh. Good morning."

She glanced from him to the photograph and back again, but her smile was bright and unrevealing when she replied, "Good morning. Were you waiting for me?"

"Yes," he said smoothly. "You're right on time."

The breakfast was the usual end-of-the-weekend gathering. Everyone looked a little tired, ready to get back to their usual routines.

The caterers were running a bit behind, and the breakfast tables weren't open yet, so groups gathered around the room and on the lanai to sip coffee and rehash the weekend. It was a smaller group than the one from last night, so the noise level was considerably lower, though there was still plenty of conversation and laughter. Nic heard several people say they were looking forward to the next reunion in five more years.

She wouldn't be around for that one, of course, but for Heidi's sake, she was glad this event had gone so well that everyone seemed to be looking forward to the next one. It seemed to mean so much to Heidi.

And speaking of Heidi…

Taking advantage of Joel being across the room, reliving a high school football game with some of his old teammates, Heidi pigeonholed Nic at the pastries table and all but dragged her out onto the lanai. "So, Nicole, did you have a nice time at our reunion?"

"Yes, I had a great time. Thanks."

"We certainly enjoyed having you here with us. It was so nice to meet one of Joel's friends from Arkansas. We all worry about him, you know. It makes us feel better to know he has people to hang out with there."

Brushing her breeze-tossed hair out of her face, Nic found herself analyzing Heidi's words, trying to read the subtext. "Joel has lots of friends," she said noncommittally.

"Oh, I'm sure he does. He always has had a way of making people love him. That's why we fret about him being happy, I suppose."

"It seems to me that everyone worries too much about Joel. He's pretty much the most self-sufficient guy I know. And one of the most content, for that matter."

Heidi patted her arm in a rather patronizing manner that set her teeth on edge. "Yes, well, you didn't see him at the last reunion or you would understand our concerns. He was in terrible shape then. Frankly I was afraid for his well-being, both emotionally and physically."

Not only did this feel entirely too much like gossip for Nic's peace of mind, but she knew how much Joel would hate having Heidi portray him as an object of pity and concern by his former classmates. "You can put your mind at ease. He's fine."

If Heidi was daunted by Nic's chilly tone, she did a good job of hiding it. "You're a good friend to him, Nicole. I'm surprised the two of you have never dated...."

The implied question mark at the end of the statement made Nic shake her head. "We've never dated," she said completely candidly. "As we've said, we're neighbors. This is the first time we've actually spent this much time together."

And doing so had led to complications neither Nic nor Joel had predicted, though she saw no reason at all to mention that to Heidi.

"Does Joel date anyone in Arkansas?" Heidi asked. "I'm not trying to snoop, really. I just want to know, as his friend, if he's getting on with his life."

"He dates when his demanding career allows. But

really, Heidi, this is sort of personal, don't you think? If you really think he wouldn't mind you asking, these are all questions you should ask Joel."

"Oh, I know, I'm coming across as really nosy," Heidi said with a little laugh. "It's just that he's so special to me. I think of him almost like a brother. And if he's making himself available, I have someone in mind that I think would be perfect for him. A cousin of my husband's. She's twenty-five, single, pretty, bright. She's a high school teacher, a former Danston High cheerleader who was valedictorian of her class. She has a master's degree in history."

"Um, Heidi—"

"She reminds me a little of Heather, actually. She wants a family, but she hasn't met anyone who was right for her yet…and I have this feeling that Joel could be the one. I'm pretty good at matchmaking, actually. I've put several successful couples together."

"Lucky them," Nic muttered.

"I'm sorry. What did you say?"

"Nothing." Nic abruptly changed the subject. "It's really nice out this morning, isn't it? Warm for October."

Heidi wasn't one to be distracted by talks of the weather. "You know Joel pretty well, being such good pals with him. How do you think he would feel if I suggested that he meet Jenny? Do you think he's ready to consider another serious relationship? Have you and he ever talked about anything like that?"

Nic was starting to get irritated. Really, *who* talked like this, outside of TV shows? It was none of her business how Joel felt about dating, and none of Heidi's either, for that matter. And if Heidi really wanted to know, anyway, she should ask Joel.

She wanted to tell Heidi in no uncertain terms that she should keep her matchmaking urges on a leash, but she bit down on her tongue to lock the acerbic words inside.

"No," she said instead, unable to keep her tone from sounding clipped. "We don't talk about things like that."

"Oh." Heidi sounded disappointed and a bit abashed. Maybe she had finally taken the hint that Nic was not going to gossip about Joel, nor give Heidi any fodder for doing so with others.

Nic half turned to look around them, searching for an excuse to escape. She and Heidi weren't the only ones taking advantage of the warm, clear morning to enjoy the view. Nearly everyone had strolled out through the open glass doors to the lanai, and cozy little groups had gathered around the railing. A brisk summer breeze tossed hair and caused white paper napkins to flutter out of inattentive hands and fly gleefully to freedom.

Suspended over the hill that sloped steeply down toward the lake, the lanai swayed a little in the breeze. No one appeared alarmed by the movement beneath their feet, nor the accompanying creaks of wood, so Nic put it out of her mind.

With a sharp gasp, Heidi suddenly caught her

arm. For a moment, Nic thought something was wrong, but then she followed the direction of Heidi's pointing finger. "Look!" Heidi said with a little squeal of pleasure. "Deer. Aren't they beautiful?"

Relieved that something besides Joel's social life held Heidi's attention now, Nic dutifully stepped forward with her to the railing, where they could both admire the deer strolling through the high grass near the lake. There were five of them, four does and a fawn, and they posed by the water in a postcard-charming tableau. Alerted by Heidi's reaction, others moved to the railing to admire the scene, so that perhaps fifteen people were gathered in one area of the lanai.

Jostled to one side, Nic smiled ruefully. One would think unicorns had just appeared out of the mist. How bored was this group that a small herd of ordinary deer could cause this sort of excitement?

She turned her head and spotted Joel and the Watson twins. Meeting her gaze, Joel smiled, and her breath caught hard in her throat. The sexy curve of his lips reminded her of how they had felt pressed against her own and ignited a strong craving to sample their taste again.

She thought suddenly of Heidi's matchmaking plans on Joel's behalf and found her fingers curling into fists at her side in response. Hastily she straightened them, smiling back at Joel.

Someone called out that the breakfast buffet was now open, and everyone forgot about the deer, moving away from the railing and toward the ballroom. Nic noticed that the Watson twins both made U-turns and headed back inside for food, though Joel stood his ground as the others swarmed past him.

He didn't look away from Nic, and she waited where she was for him to join her. She didn't think he would mind being at the back of the line, and she wouldn't mind a few minutes alone with him out in this lovely setting.

"Nicole." Maybe Heidi had noticed that intimate exchange of smiles and was deliberately trying to interrupt. She hadn't moved away from the railing. "Come look. The little fawn is so cute."

Dragging her gaze from Joel's, Nic turned obediently to take a step toward the other woman.

She felt the quiver of the wood only moments before the floor beneath her feet seemed to shift. And then one corner of the lanai—the corner closest to where Heidi stood—simply collapsed.

Someone screamed behind her. Heidi stumbled, her arms flailing. Feeling the wood shift beneath her again, Nic was instantly aware that she should throw herself backward, toward safety.

She shot forward instead, toward Heidi and the crumbling corner of the lanai.

Joel was walking toward Nic, his pulse thumping at the base of his throat in response to the smile they'd exchanged, when the deck collapsed. His heart stopped altogether when he saw her stumble toward the broken edge of the two-story lanai. She caught herself immediately, but then, to his horror, threw herself directly toward the break.

The lanai shuddered again beneath him and people began to scream behind him. He surged forward, calling Nic's name.

He saw her grab Heidi and all but shove her toward Joel. Joel managed to catch Heidi without stumbling, and he acted on pure instinct when he half turned to push her toward the doors and safety. She fell, but Ernie Watson caught her arm and half-pulled, half-dragged her inside.

Nic threw herself toward Joel the moment she was certain that Heidi was safe, but the collapsing foundation had started a chain reaction that made the whole lanai start to crumble. She stumbled and slid backward as the wood sloped beneath her.

It all happened in a fraction of a second, but Joel felt as though he were watching Nic fall in slow motion.

"Nic!" he shouted again, reaching for her.

She jumped toward him. He made a desperate grab, but his grasping fingers closed around empty air. Someone latched on to him from behind just as the lanai split again with a loud crack. Even as he struggled against the force pulling him back toward the doors, Nic tumbled over the broken edge and out of his sight.

Nic's head hurt. She didn't often wake with a headache, she thought without opening her eyes. And why did the rest of her body feel so stiff and sore?

Her bed felt odd. Hard. Lumpy. Strange noises surrounded her, and an acrid antiseptic scent tickled her nose. Some part of her mind was aware that she wasn't in her own bedroom, but she was having trouble making her eyelids open so that she could figure out exactly what was going on.

"Nic?"

Joel's voice. She latched on to the familiar sound and tried to force her eyes open. She wanted to see him.

Her vision was blurred. His face was seriously out of focus as he leaned over her, saying her name again. She blinked rapidly—or tried to. It seemed as though even her eyelids were moving slowly. "Joel?"

What was that funny croak? Surely not her voice. She cleared her throat, then winced when another bolt of pain shot through her head.

"Hey," he said softly, very lightly brushing a strand of hair away from her face. "You're awake. How do you feel?"

"I, um…" Her mind was still hazy, the words hard to retrieve, but she was relieved to see that his face was slowly coming into focus. He was smiling, though his eyes were very grave. "I'm okay. Where…?"

"You're in the hospital, but you're going to be okay," he assured her quickly. "You fell. Remember? The lanai collapsed. Some sort of structural defect."

Though he was still smiling at her, she heard an underlying fierceness in his voice. She'd rarely seen Joel angry, but something about his tone made her glad it wasn't directed at her.

"Is everyone else okay?" she asked as the memories began to creep back into her aching head. "Heidi?"

Joel's smile broadened. "Heidi's out in the waiting room, telling everyone in sight that you are a hero. She says you saved her life with your quick thinking. She'll probably cry all over you the minute she has a chance."

Nic grimaced. "That's really not necessary," she said fervently.

He gave her a sympathetic pat on the shoulder. "I'll hold her off as long as I can."

"Thanks." Shifting on the bed, she winced again when her movement tugged at the IV taped to her left hand and sent shooting pains through various parts of her body. "Was anyone else hurt?"

"Earl Watson twisted an ankle when he made a grab for me when the lanai collapsed. He was still able to hold on to a doorway and keep us both from going over after you. Heidi skinned her knees when she fell scrambling to get inside, but she's fine. Everyone else had just gone inside for breakfast when the structure gave way. We don't know whether it was already broken while they were standing out on the deck or gave way just as they moved inward."

"It's sort of coming back to me now. I remember the lanai falling and I sort of remember being in an ambulance."

"It's natural that you would have some memory gaps. You have a concussion."

"A concussion. Okay. Anything else?"

"Quite a few bruises. You've got six stitches just

under your chin—you'll have a scar, but it'll fade to a very thin line, barely noticeable, with time."

Wiggling her jaw tentatively and feeling the gauze taped to her chin, she nodded. She wasn't worried about a scar—she had several of those already.

"You've got some other minor cuts, none of them deep enough for stitches, and you'll have some spectacular bruises. A particularly nasty bruise on your right shoulder, where you took the brunt of the fall. For the next few days you're going to feel like you were beaten up, but that's the extent of it. You were very lucky that you landed on a slope and rolled rather than hitting a solid surface and having debris fall on top of you."

She sort of remembered Joel getting to her while she'd lain on the ground, dazed and not yet feeling the pain that would hit in the ambulance. He'd sounded frantic when he'd said her name, more rattled than she'd ever seen him. He'd have felt the same way about any of his friends, of course, but she remembered how safe she had felt at knowing he was nearby and watching out for her.

"No broken bones?" she asked just for reassurance.

"No, thank goodness. Anyone else might have been badly hurt after a ten-foot drop, but I've always said you were the toughest woman I know."

She smiled faintly. "And don't you forget it."

"Not likely." He leaned over to brush a kiss across her forehead. "You scared the stuffing out of me."

"Yeah, well, that's what I was hoping to do," she

murmured, letting her heavy eyelids drift downward again. "I've been planning it all weekend. Just to make the reunion a little more exciting, you know."

He chuckled softly, but there was an odd little catch in the sound. "Next time let's just keep things nice and dull, okay?"

She started to tell him that there wouldn't be a next time. By the time his next class reunion rolled around, she and Joel would be living different and very likely separate lives. But suddenly it just seemed like too much trouble to try to form the words. She made a murmuring sound and closed her eyes.

Joel brushed her hair back again, his fingertips barely touching her skin. "Why don't you get some rest? I'll be close by if you need me."

That reassuring thought made it easier for her to slide into sleep, the feel of his light touch on her forehead overriding the pains assaulting the rest of her body.

Chapter Eleven

Even though he hadn't been hurt in the lanai collapse, Joel ached all over as he walked slowly to the waiting room. He dreaded what waited for him there and would have preferred to be alone for a little while to process everything that had happened that morning.

No such luck, of course. Heidi limped toward him the moment he appeared in the waiting room doorway, her face pale, her eyes huge. "Joel? How is she?"

"She's going to be fine, Heidi. She was very lucky."

"Lucky?" Heidi pressed a hand to her generously rounded chest. "How can you say that after she took that terrible fall?"

"She's banged up some, but she's going to be okay. Trust me, it could have been a whole lot worse."

"She saved my life. She could have jumped to safety, but she grabbed me instead."

She had been saying words to that effect almost without stopping since the lanai fell. "She's a cop, Heidi. She's trained to jump into dangerous situations when others are at risk. She would have done the same for anyone."

Heidi shook her head. "As grateful as I am to Nicole, I'm glad you and she are only friends, Joel. I can't imagine you living every day with the anxiety of worrying about her safety, especially when she doesn't seem to think twice about throwing herself into hazardous situations. First the fight at the game and then this morning…it's a miracle that she hasn't been seriously hurt yet."

For someone who proclaimed herself undyingly grateful to Nic, Heidi seemed awfully critical. But maybe he was just getting a little cranky.

"Why don't you head on home, Heidi? I'm sure you could use a rest. Nic's going to be sleeping for a while, so she really doesn't need visitors. I'll tell her you were here to check on her."

Heidi's husband stepped forward to take her arm. "He's right, honey. Let's go home so you can take a long bath and soak those sore knees. Joel will make sure his friend is cared for properly."

Reluctantly Heidi allowed herself to be drawn away after giving Joel Nic's canvas tote bag, which

Heidi had been keeping safe. Joel spent the next ten minutes dispersing other friends who had gathered in the waiting room to make sure everyone was okay.

It was with a great sense of relief that he watched the Watson twins and their wives, the last of the group, move away. They had made him promise to call them if he needed anything at all, but he doubted that it would be necessary.

Looking forward to a few minutes of solitude, he turned—only to come face-to-face with his brother. "Ethan. What are you doing here?"

Ethan motioned toward a couple of empty chairs in one relatively quiet corner of the waiting room. "Mom called me. She thought you'd want someone to keep you company. She and Dad thought about coming themselves, but I told them to sit tight and I'd keep them updated."

"Thanks." Joel was frankly relieved that his parents hadn't come. His father was much too restless to sit still for long in a waiting room, and his pacing and grumbling would eventually get on everyone's nerves. As for Elaine, she was such a worrier that she'd be wringing her hands and fretting—and getting on Joel's nerves. As much as he loved them, his folks weren't exactly the rock-solid types during times of trouble.

Ethan was just the opposite. His calm, practical demeanor was a reassuring presence during any crisis. Joel couldn't remember the last time he'd seen his older brother truly rattled by anything life threw at them. Their mother worried sometimes that Ethan suppressed too much, cutting himself off from the joys of life as well as the anguish. But who was to say Ethan's way wasn't better in the long run?

"You want some coffee or something?" Ethan asked as they took their seats. He motioned toward a couple of carafes in one corner of the room, maintained by hospital volunteers.

"No, I'm good. Get some for yourself if you want."

Ethan shook his head. "How's Nic? Mom made it sound like she was on her deathbed, but the nurses said that she's going to be okay."

Joel summed up Nic's injuries, adding the same sentiment he had expressed to Heidi. "She was lucky."

"Damned lucky," Ethan agreed. "That could have been a tragedy—for a lot of people. It's a wonder Nic was the only one who fell when the balcony collapsed."

"No kidding. Nearly a dozen people had been standing in that corner only minutes before it buckled. I don't know what caused the supports to collapse just as they rushed inside for breakfast— whether it was the movement or the shifting weight or what—but Heidi and Nic were the ones left behind and in the most danger of falling."

"Is it true that Nic pushed Heidi away from the edge?"

"Yeah. She grabbed her and shoved her away just as the railing snapped. Her reflexes were amazing, Ethan. Before I'd even had time to realize what was happening, Nic had already grabbed Heidi and all but thrown her toward me. She never even thought about her own safety, she just jumped right toward the edge to help Heidi."

"That's what she's trained to do, isn't it? Put herself into danger to help other people."

Heidi had said something similar in reference to Nic's job. And while Joel had never really worried too much about Nic's career before, figuring she was hardly keeping the peace in a dangerous urban setting, suddenly he found himself looking at it a little differently. It took a certain personality to be a police officer—bold, determined, maybe even a little reckless—and Nic fit that profile a little too well.

That was something he was going to have to think about later, in private.

The cheery opening tones of "Here Comes the Sun" caught his attention, making him look around with a frown. The sound was coming from Nic's canvas tote bag, which he'd dropped on the empty chair beside him.

He debated whether he should try to dig out the phone and answer it. It could be one of her family members, in which case he would have to explain what had happened to her and pass along reassurances that she would recover fully. Yet for some reason he thought the caller might be Aislinn. And since she had already expressed concerns about Nic this weekend, he knew she would worry if no one answered the call.

He sighed and dug through the daunting assortment of junk in Nic's bag to find the phone. The ringtone was still playing when he located it, then held it to his ear. "Hello?"

After a very brief pause he heard, "Oh. Joel. It's Aislinn."

So his hunch had been correct. He supposed he should be relieved that it wasn't Nic's mother. Nic would probably want to tell her family about the accident in her own way. But Aislinn still made him a little nervous. "Hi, Aislinn."

"Is everything okay there?"

Aware of Ethan listening in, Joel said, "Nic's been hurt, but she's going to be okay."

A longer pause followed his words this time. "She'll be all right?"

There was no surprise at all in her voice that something had happened. Just a need for reassurance that her friend wasn't badly injured. Joel shook his head a little even as he repeated, "She'll be fine. She has a concussion and some bruises and she's being kept in the hospital today for observation, but there's no reason to think we won't be able to come home tomorrow."

"What happened?"

He gave her a quick summary of the accident, finishing with, "It could have been a hell of a lot worse."

He could almost hear Aislinn shudder. "Yes. I wish I'd had a better sense of what was going to happen. All I knew is that Nic was in some sort of danger. I wasn't any help to her at all."

"Aislinn, how could you have known that balcony

was going to collapse? You would have had to have been...well, you know."

"I know." She sighed heavily. "What good are better-than-average intuitions if they don't actually keep your friends from being injured anyway?"

Because that seemed to be a rhetorical question—and one he couldn't have answered if it wasn't—Joel said simply, "I'll have Nic call you as soon as she's rested a bit, okay? You'll feel a lot better once you've talked to her and convinced yourself she's all right."

"Thank you, Joel. Is there anything I can do? Should I come there to help?"

"No. My brother's here with me now, and my parents are available if we need them for anything. But thank you for offering."

"Take care of Nic, Joel."

"I will," he promised.

"And let your brother help you. He needs to feel useful."

"I, uh—"

But Aislinn had already disconnected, leaving him shaking his head in bemusement.

Ethan was looking at him oddly when Joel dropped the phone back in Nic's bag, and he was glad his brother hadn't heard Aislinn's parting advice.

"That was Nic's friend, Aislinn Flaherty."

"The psychic?" Ethan's lip curled a bit as he said the word.

"She doesn't claim to be psychic. She just has...feelings."

"And she had a feeling something happened to Nic?"

"Yes."

Ethan shook his head in open disbelief. "Bull."

Joel shrugged. "Well, she has been calling all weekend worrying that something bad was going to happen."

"Doesn't prove anything. Maybe she calls all the time with veiled warnings. She'd have to be right every once in a while."

"No." Joel shook his head. "That isn't Aislinn at all. You'd have to meet her to understand, but you've got her all wrong."

"I'm not interested in meeting her. She sounds like a crackpot. But never mind about that. What's your plan now? You said they're keeping Nic overnight?"

"Probably. She'll be watched closely today, but if everything looks good, there's no reason to think she won't be released tomorrow morning. I need to call and reschedule our flight for tomorrow afternoon. I know Nic will want to go home as soon as possible. I guess I should call the police department and let them know she won't be at work for a few days. I should have asked Aislinn to do that."

"Yeah, that would have been a helpful thing for her to do," Ethan muttered. "Rather than calling once a day with predictions of doom."

Joel wasn't in the mood to argue with his brother about Aislinn at the moment. It wouldn't accomplish anything anyway. "I'm glad everyone else finally went home for a while. Heidi will probably be back, but I needed some time to take care of details without all those other people hovering around."

"Have you heard from the resort management yet?"

"Yes. The owner made me promise to call him if Nic needed anything at all."

"I'm sure his first call was to his lawyer," Ethan said cynically. "Nic won't have to worry about any of these medical bills and she'll probably get some sort of settlement for pain and suffering. Someone's going to have to take responsibility for that balcony collapse, especially considering that the number of people using it this morning was well within safe limits."

Joel shrugged off talk of liability and settlements. "We'll let their lawyers and Nic's lawyer handle all that stuff. I've got more immediate concerns to attend to. And speaking of which, I'd better start making those calls. Nic probably has her work number stored in her phone."

"What can I do to help?"

Remembering Aislinn's comment that Ethan needed to feel useful—and what the heck had made her say that anyway?—Joel gave it only a moment's thought before replying, "I never did get breakfast this morning. If you could round me up a muffin or something…"

"I'm on it." Ethan was on his feet with an alacrity that made Joel suspect that Aislinn had been right on target again. His head now aching in earnest, he dug for Nic's phone again.

* * *

Nic had never been so happy to walk into her own bedroom as she was when Joel escorted her in late Monday afternoon. Though her head was aching and she was sore all over, she moved quickly and without limping, determined to show Joel that she was well on her way to full recovery.

He hadn't exactly hovered over her during their trip home, probably knowing how much she would hate it if he did, but she'd been aware that he'd watched her closely. In response, she'd been even more determined to show no weakness, so that now she was about ready to collapse.

She wouldn't, however, until she was alone. And it didn't look as if that was going to be anytime soon, since Joel was still right at her heels. He set her bag down at the foot of her bed. "You should get some rest. Maybe have a cup of hot herbal tea first. It will help you relax."

She managed a smile. "That sounds great. I'll probably do just that."

His smile was much too knowing as he raised a hand to cup her cheek. "What would really help you relax is for me to get out of here and leave you alone. But I'd like to stay just a little while longer, if you don't mind too badly, just to make sure you'll be okay after that tiring trip home."

"Of course I don't mind. You can join me for a cup of that tea you mentioned," she said, her skin feeling suddenly warm beneath his touch.

Maybe she was developing a fever. Or maybe

she'd been suffering from this particular fever for longer than she'd been willing to admit, she thought ruefully, resisting the impulse to nestle her cheek into his hand.

His smile faded as their eyes locked. "I haven't told you yet how sorry I am about what happened. If I'd had any idea that anything like that would happen, I never would have dragged you to my reunion."

Touched by the genuine regret in his expression, she lifted her hand to cover his on her cheek. "How could you have known? Aislinn's as close to being psychic as anyone we know and even she wasn't able to warn us not to go out on the lanai. I certainly don't blame you, Joel."

His thumb slid along the ridge of her cheekbone, just above the edge of the gauze bandage on her chin. "I haven't told you how frightened I was when I saw you go over that edge. You scared the hell out of me."

"You forgot that I'm in pretty good shape," she reminded him. "I know how to take a fall."

"You aren't Superwoman. You could have been badly hurt. Or worse."

"But I wasn't. A few bruises and a few days off work. No biggie."

"You must be sorry I ever mentioned my reunion."

"Actually, it was an…interesting experience." She couldn't think of a better adjective, but she supposed that one summed it up well enough.

His lopsided smile expressed his own mixed emotions. "I suppose that's one way of putting it."

She couldn't resist tilting her head just a little,

rubbing her cheek against his hand in the process. "You're probably the one who's sorry Aislinn ever came up with the idea of taking me to your reunion. It hardly turned out the way you'd planned."

"Not exactly, no." And then he lowered his head toward hers. "Some things are better when you don't plan them," he murmured just before his mouth covered hers.

Simply because she wanted to, Nic wrapped both arms around his neck. Her bruised right shoulder screamed a protest of the movement, but she ignored it. Anything that felt this good was worth a little accompanying pain.

Careful of her bruises, Joel gathered her closer, his hands sliding around her waist to spread across her back. His palms were warm through the fabric of her pullover top.

Though her mind was beginning to cloud, Nic clearly remembered how it had felt to dance with him for the first time. So natural. So right. As if they had danced together many times before.

Kissing him felt much the same to her. As if she'd been wanting to kiss him for a very long time. As if kissing him had been inevitable from the day they'd first met.

He released her mouth long enough to draw a deep, sharp breath and then he kissed her again, more deeply this time. There had been wonder in their earlier kisses. Daring. Maybe even a bit of rebellion against all the people who had warned them away from each other—including themselves.

This time there was passion. And a growing hunger Nic wasn't sure they would be able to ignore for much longer.

She was finding it harder with each passing moment to remember why they should try.

He lifted his head very slowly, ending the kiss with an obvious reluctance. He didn't release her but pressed his forehead to hers, his voice rough when he said, "I should probably stop doing that."

Every nerve ending in her body rebelling at the very suggestion, she lifted her mouth to his again. "Don't stop on my behalf."

The kiss they shared then was hot enough to almost melt the soles of her boots.

Somehow they ended up on her bed. Maybe later she would remember which one of them had initiated that move, but for now she was too busy enjoying the feel of his hands on her body, his lips against hers. His hands were eager, avid as they raced over her—and yet his touch was gentle, almost tender, so careful not to cause her any discomfort from her assorted scrapes and bruises.

As if she could feel anything but pleasure at that moment, she thought with a low moan.

He stilled. "Am I hurting you?"

"Are you kidding? Has anybody ever told you you've got magical hands?" She closed her eyes and concentrated fully on the springy feel of his hair around her fingers. The solid weight of him pressed against her from chest to thigh. The masculine warmth seeping through his shirt and jeans. The hardness pressed so blatantly against her hip.

Wow, she thought in a daze of arousal. This was Joel. Her neighbor, her friend. And he wanted her. Wanted her badly, apparently. And she wanted him so much that she ached with it. Who'd have thought their friendly trip to his class reunion would lead to this?

Anyone with any sense at all, she answered herself with a flash of candid insight. This attraction had been building for some time. Part of her had been aware of it, to the point that she'd worried that going with him to his hometown would lead to something that might put their friendship at risk.

She still worried about that even as she opened her mouth beneath his again. But it was too late now to try to deny, to either of them, the way she felt about him.

She slid her hands beneath the hem of his shirt, spreading her fingers and pressing her palms against his skin. Remembering the way he had looked coming out of the shower damp and bare-chested, she was delighted to discover that he felt every bit as good as he had looked. She traced ribs and muscles with her fingertips, lingering at the dip in his back just above the top of his jeans.

Joel groaned. "We'd better…"

She silenced him by slipping her tongue between his lips, letting herself savor and explore at her leisure.

A long time later Joel tried again to be sensible. "Nic, we should stop," he muttered against her throat.

She snuggled against him, feeling the evidence

that he was no more eager to put an end to this than she was. "Why?"

The simple question seemed to catch him off guard. He lifted his head. "Why? Well, uh, because…"

She smiled and rubbed a fingertip along his moist lower lip. "Not much of a reason, Brannon."

"We said we were going to take this slow, remember? Careful."

"We'll be careful. And we can take it as slowly as you like."

Her wicked tone made him groan and shift restlessly against her again. "You aren't helping."

"Then let me make it easy for you." She cupped his face between her hands, letting him see the sincerity in her expression. "It's like you said the first time you kissed me, in your car by the lake—this has been coming for a long time. Maybe it will work out, maybe it won't, but since neither of us has a crystal ball, I don't want to fret about a future we can't predict."

"Just live in the moment, huh? Take each day as it comes?"

"Do we really have any other choice? Who knows what's going to happen tomorrow?"

It was a philosophy she'd lived by for a long time. In the long run, she figured it prevented a lot of angst and distress. Maybe Joel was going to break her heart at the end of this venture or maybe he wasn't— but they might as well enjoy the journey while it lasted.

She'd had a good time with Brad, hadn't she? And she'd gotten over being dumped by him easily enough, choosing to concentrate on the parts of her life that she could control. Like her work and her friends.

A tiny voice inside her whispered that Joel wasn't Brad. That her feelings for Brad hadn't been quite this strong or this risky. That it might not be so easy to move on this time. Firmly ignoring that annoying nagging, she smiled up at Joel, waiting for him to make his decision.

He sighed. "We don't know what will happen tomorrow, do we?"

"Nope. Even Aislinn's only right some of the time. The rest of us just have to play it by ear."

His hand on her cheek, his eyes locked with hers, Joel resisted only a moment longer before gathering her close again.

Chapter Twelve

He didn't try to hold anything back this time. His kisses grew hotter, his movements more purposeful, until they were both gasping and writhing in growing hunger. Nic pulled away from him only long enough to retrieve a small cardboard box from her nightstand, putting it near at hand, and then she reached for the hem of his long-sleeve polo shirt, tugging it up and over his head.

His face creased in concentration, Joel followed suit, stripping her out of her clothing with an efficiency that rather impressed her. His fingertips traced tenderly over her bruises. "You should be resting," he murmured.

"I will," she promised, pressing herself against

him, hearing his breath catch hard in his throat as bare skin brushed bare skin. "Later."

And she covered his mouth with her own again, pushing him backward into the pillows.

To make it as comfortable for her as possible, Joel allowed Nic to set the pace of their lovemaking. She was the one who urged him to settle between her legs, who made it clear that she was feeling no pain. At least not enough to concern either of them.

She was the one who raised to welcome him when he couldn't wait any longer to enter her. And she was the one who stiffened and cried out when she reached a pinnacle of pleasure that seemed higher than any peak she'd ever climbed before.

This time Joel tumbled eagerly over the edge with her.

There was something about the sound of Joel's rapid heartbeat beneath her ear. The feel of strong arms around her. The slight tickle of a lightly furred chest against her cheek. The lazy heaviness of sated limbs. She sighed in satisfaction and snuggled a bit more deeply into Joel's shoulder.

"What's wrong? Are you hurting?"

She patted his chest in response to his anxious question. "I'm fine. Better than fine, actually. I was just enjoying the moment."

He relaxed a little, though she thought she detected a lingering tension in his muscles. "You really should get some rest. You just got out of the hospital this morning."

"There was no reason at all for me to spend last night in the hospital, and you know it. It was only a mild concussion. The doctors were just being over cautious—and I think you had some influence over that."

"I just wanted to make sure you didn't have any problems crop up during the night. I know concussions are fairly common, but they're nothing to take lightly. You probably have a headache right now, even though I know you won't complain about it."

She shrugged. "Maybe a little headache. I've had worse."

He shifted her to one side and moved toward the edge of the bed. "I'll get you a couple of ibuprofen. And you never had that herbal tea we talked about."

She laughed softly. "That was supposed to help me relax. I think you took care of that already."

"Glad to be of service."

She had been too comfortable and content to notice before that something was bothering Joel. Now she saw that his smile looked strained and did not reach his eyes. His shoulders looked stiff, and a muscle twitched in his jaw.

Not the face of a man who was floating on a haze of postlovemaking satisfaction, she thought with a sudden frown. "Something wrong?"

"No, of course not." But he didn't meet her gaze as he spoke. Scooping his jeans off the floor, he asked over his shoulder, "You keep ibuprofen in the bathroom?"

"Yes. In the medicine cabinet."

After he disappeared into the bathroom, she climbed slowly out of the bed and pulled a short terry robe out of her closet. Perhaps she had understated her headache a bit, she thought, lightly rubbing her temples. And maybe she was more sore and stiff than she wanted him to know.

She wondered what Joel's problem was.

When he finally emerged, he was mostly dressed and carrying two tablets and a glass of water. "Here. Take these."

She complied, then said, "Why don't I make us that tea now?"

"You know, I really should take my bags into my house and then shower and run by the clinic for a little while, since I'm a day later getting home than I expected. Unless you need me for anything here?"

She shook her head. "I'll be fine. But—"

He was already inching toward the door. "D'you want me to call Aislinn to come stay with you for a while?"

"No, thanks. She'll probably show up before long anyway."

"Okay, then. You'll call me if you need anything? Anything at all?"

"Of course. Joel—"

He paused with one foot already out the doorway. "Yeah?"

"Are we ever going to talk about this?"

His cheeks went a little red, and he swallowed, obviously embarrassed by his own behavior. "Yeah, sure. We'll, uh, talk later. I'll see you, okay?"

Despite the jumbled emotions inside her, she managed to smile. "Whenever you're ready."

He hesitated a moment longer, then turned and left. Shortly afterward she heard her front door close.

Joel was cute even in full panic mode, she thought a bit wistfully. The question was, what had made him take off that way, looking as though he was running for his life?

"Do you need anything else? More lasagna? Another roll?"

Nic shook her head in response to Aislinn's offer and she was pleased to note that the movement caused hardly any discomfort in response. The dull headache that had plagued her much of the day was mostly gone now. A long, hot shower followed by a restful nap had eased some of the soreness that had resulted from the exertions of the day—traveling home from Alabama and handing her heart over to Joel on a shiny silver platter, she thought with a wry twist of her mouth.

"I'm really full," she said, pushing thoughts of Joel to the back of her mind for the moment. "But the dinner was wonderful. It was so nice of you to go to the trouble of bringing it over."

Aislinn shrugged. "It was the least I could do. I haven't been much help to you otherwise this past weekend."

"What do you mean?"

"I wasn't able to warn you about the lanai."

"Which only proves that you aren't the psychic Pamela keeps telling everyone you are. You had a feeling there was going to be a problem and you checked on me several times. I know you were concerned about me."

Aislinn didn't look significantly comforted. "I was the one who suggested to Joel that he should take you to the reunion. I shouldn't have gotten involved. Matchmaking is always risky, especially when you're setting up your best friend."

"You couldn't have known I would get hurt at the reunion. You were just trying to help Joel with a problem—after he asked us to offer suggestions," Nic reminded her.

And then it struck her exactly what Aislinn had said. "Wait a minute. Matchmaking? You were matchmaking?"

Her face flushed, Aislinn nodded apologetically. "I thought it would be a chance for you and Joel to get out of the comfortable routines you'd fallen into and explore the possibilities between you. Now I wonder if I made a mistake."

"Why exactly?" Nic wasn't sure she wanted the answer, but she felt compelled to ask.

Aislinn cleared her throat. "Would you like some dessert? I brought brownies."

"I'll have dessert later. First I want to know why you think it was a mistake to try to put Joel and me together. Do you have one of your feelings about it?"

Looking miserable, Aislinn crumbled the remains of a crusty roll onto her plate. "Not exactly. I'm just afraid you're going to be hurt again. And I don't mean physically this time."

She really shouldn't have asked, Nic thought with a sinking feeling inside her chest. Aislinn was pretty much predicting disaster from Nic and Joel's new relationship. And because that opinion was a bit too close to Nic's own concerns, she felt any lingering optimism about this latest development with Joel start to slip away.

"You don't have to worry about me," she said, deliberately injecting a touch of bravado into her voice. "I know better than to let that happen."

"Do you?" Aislinn murmured, and her expression made Nic suspect that Aislinn knew exactly what had transpired between her and Joel earlier that day.

She sighed. "Maybe not."

Aislinn set down her fork. "Do you want to talk about it?"

"I wouldn't know where to begin."

"Tell me about the weekend."

"I wouldn't know where to start there, either."

"Why not at the beginning?"

That seemed like a reasonable suggestion. After all, she and Aislinn had always told each other almost everything that happened to them.

She started talking, describing her arrival in Alabama, meeting Joel's brother and parents, attending the football game dressed in the opposing team's colors, lunch with Ethan the next day, the dance, the kisses by the lake, all the way up to the collapse of the lanai. If she left anything out, it wasn't intentional. After all, she figured, Aislinn would probably sense anything she tried to hide.

She stopped the narrative at the point where she and Joel had walked into her house that afternoon. Maybe Aislinn had already guessed what happened after that, but Nic wasn't quite ready to talk about it.

Aislinn had listened in attentive silence, but now she asked, "You said Joel's parents saw you off this morning. How did they react to your being injured?"

"Oh, they were very sympathetic. Really distressed about the whole thing, as if it reflected badly on their hospitality. And managing to imply that it wouldn't have happened if I hadn't been such a reckless type."

"Oh, surely they didn't—"

Nic held up a hand. "That was unfair of me," she admitted. "They were perfectly gracious. They even gave me a beautiful box of chocolates when I left. I'm being a jerk when I should be grateful for their kindness and hospitality. I promise I'll write a thank-you note to them before I go to bed tonight and I'll put it in the mail first thing in the morning."

"Nic, have I ever judged you?" Aislinn looked at her reprovingly from across the table. "You can tell me exactly how they made you feel, whether it was intentional on their part or not."

Nic sighed and pushed a hand through her hair. "I know. I just hate hearing myself sounding so petty. Yes, that was the way I felt with them, but I wouldn't say they 'made' me feel that way. I can't help wondering how much I was projecting my own feelings onto them."

"You somehow blame yourself for being hurt?"

"Not exactly. I mean, you always think you should have reacted faster or differently or something, but I wouldn't have left Heidi to fall, regardless. I knew I was more prepared to go over than she was, since she was less aware of what was happening. And I'm in much better shape than she is," she added with typical candor, knowing Aislinn would take it as fact rather than boasting.

"Not to mention that you're trained to help other people, not to protect yourself."

"Well, yeah. That's my job. And I hated that I felt I was being judged because of it. *It doesn't sound like a job for a young lady,*" she paraphrased primly. "Not like, oh, say, family counseling."

"Family counseling?" Aislinn repeated in a murmur, watching her too intently.

Nic flushed and looked down into her tea glass, which now held more melted ice than beverage. She knew her next words would tell Aislinn a great deal and she wondered for a moment if she was ready to reveal quite that much. Yet still she said them. "That was Heather's career. Joel's wife."

"I see."

"She must have been an amazing woman. Everyone loved her. Her in-laws. Her classmates. The whole world apparently loved Heather."

"Surely there were other girls in her class who didn't care for her. Who were jealous of her or just didn't get along with her."

"If there were, they knew better than to say anything at the reunion. They would have been stoned."

"Nic."

"Okay, that was an exaggeration. Let's just say that any criticism of Heather would have been strongly discouraged." She told Aislinn about the scholarship, which they both agreed was a wonderful gesture, and about the photo shrine to Heather in Elaine's upstairs hallway, which was a bit more thought-provoking.

Aislinn pushed her plate aside, propped her elbow on the table and rested her chin in her hand, looking thoughtful. "Anytime someone passes away tragically young, there's a tendency to sort of turn them into saints in the memories of those who knew them."

"True. But it's awfully difficult to follow in the footsteps of a saint."

"It would be daunting," Aislinn agreed. "But maybe Joel isn't looking for a saint this time."

"Or maybe he isn't looking at all," Nic muttered, remembering the way he had all but bolted from her house earlier.

"He's looking. The question is whether he's really seeing clearly."

Aislinn didn't often fall into cryptic, psychic-style speech, and when she did, Nic didn't let her get away with it. Her typical reaction was to tease and scoff until Aislinn either admitted she didn't know an answer or was more clear about what her intuition told her. This time she hesitated before following up on Aislinn's comment. Maybe there was something inside her that didn't want to examine Aislinn's feelings too closely when it came to her and Joel.

Just as she was about to speak, Aislinn stood and reached for the dirty dishes. "I'll clean up the kitchen. You go into the den and rest a while and I'll bring you some hot tea when I'm done."

Nic rose, shaking her head. "I'm not an invalid. I can help—"

"Nic." Aislinn walked around to lay a hand on Nic's arm. "Let me do this. Even though I know you don't blame me, I still feel guilty for urging you to go to Alabama. I feel as if I set you up to be hurt—in several ways. I didn't know until too late that I was putting you at risk. Just…let me take care of you tonight, okay? We can go back to normal tomorrow."

Nic didn't quite know what to say. Her throat had tightened in response to the emotion in Aislinn's voice.

She didn't want to imagine what it would be like to lose Aislinn and she knew that went both ways. It must have been awful for Aislinn to somehow sense that Nic was in danger and not be able to do anything to prevent it. So, as much as she disliked being hovered over and as determined as she was to convince Aislinn that she bore no responsibility for Nic's accident, she supposed she could give in just this once and let Aislinn clean her kitchen.

Joel stood on Nic's front porch, a package in one hand and his heart in his throat. He felt like an idiot for the way he'd run out on her earlier. He had taken to his heels in panic and he was quite sure Nic knew

it. Now he felt awkward and uncertain and uncomfortable, emotions he'd never expected to feel around
Nic, of all people.

This was exactly what he'd worried about, he
thought with a frown. He'd been afraid of ruining a
friendship that had meant a great deal to him. He
hoped he hadn't done so yet.

He was surprised when Aislinn opened the door
to him, rather than Nic. He'd known she was here,
of course, because he had seen her car parked in the
driveway, but Nic usually answered her own door.
"Oh, hi. Is Nic okay?"

"She's fine," Aislinn assured him with a smile
that looked oddly strained. "I was just leaving. Nice
seeing you, Joel."

The words lacked a measure of sincerity. He
looked at her more closely, but her face was closed
to him. "It's, um, good to see you, too."

She nodded and stepped past him. "Good night."

One hand on Nic's doorknob, Joel turned.
"Aislinn—"

She looked over her shoulder. "What?"

He didn't quite know how to ask. "Is there a
problem?"

Her expression didn't change. "I don't know. Is
there?"

"Are you annoyed with me?"

"Not yet."

He sighed. "Are you trying to send me a message?
Because if you are, I'm not getting it."

She made a gesture that expressed the same sort

of frustration he was feeling. "I'm not trying to send you any messages, Joel. I don't have any messages for you. I certainly don't have all the answers. I just...don't want Nic to be hurt any more."

"Neither do I."

She shrugged. "Then we're agreed. Good night."

He watched her open her car door. "It was your idea for me to take her with me, you know," he couldn't resist calling out.

With one foot already in the car, she looked at him. "Was it?"

Wincing, he realized that he was the one who had actually suggested Nic go with him. "Well...you didn't talk her out of it," he muttered, feeling stupid even as the words left him.

Apparently deciding that wasn't worth a response, Aislinn climbed into her car and slammed the door.

"Joel?"

In response to Nic's voice, he turned again, hearing Aislinn drive away behind him. Drawing a deep breath, he pushed the door open and walked inside.

She was standing in the living room, looking as though she'd just risen from the couch, maybe to find out what was taking him so long to come inside. "Hi. Were you talking to Aislinn?"

"Yeah. I'm not exactly her favorite person right now."

"I didn't tell her what happened between us," Nic assured him quickly, a bit defensively.

While he was relieved to hear that, it didn't

convince him that Aislinn hadn't put two and two together. She seemed to have already decided that Joel was going to break Nic's heart. Ironically enough, Joel was more concerned that it was going to end up the other way around.

"How are you feeling?" he asked.

Nic shrugged. "Fine. My head isn't even hurting now."

She didn't look fine with the gauze taped to her chin and the bruises on her cheek and arms, but she still looked entirely too appealing to him. Clearing his throat, he asked, "Did you eat?"

"Yes. Aislinn brought dinner for me. There are leftovers in the fridge if you're hungry."

"No, thanks. I grabbed a sandwich earlier. Oh, I brought you this."

Looking curious, she accepted the brown paper bag from him. He should have thought to make a nicer presentation, he realized belatedly. A bow or some ribbon or something. Just because Nic had been his friend for so long didn't mean she didn't deserve some of the little niceties of courtship now that their relationship had changed.

The smile she gave him after looking inside the bag told him she liked the gift despite the stark presentation. "Chocolate-dipped dried fruits. You remembered I love these."

"You might have mentioned it once or twice."

"Thank you, Joel. I'll enjoy these. They'll help me pass the time until I can go back to work."

"Getting antsy already?"

"Definitely. What am I supposed to do with myself all day for the rest of the week? I hate daytime TV."

"Don't you have any hobbies you've been neglecting for lack of time?"

She wrinkled her nose. "Work is my hobby. Same as you."

She had him there, he had to acknowledge as they sat side by side on the couch. "I guess we need to talk about what happened earlier."

Her bandaged chin thrust forward in challenge as she tilted her head. "That depends. Are you going to tell me you're sorry you took off the way you did or that we made a huge mistake?"

He sensed that she was hiding any vulnerability behind this air of bravado. Just as she wouldn't let him know about any pain she might be feeling from her injuries, she would deliberately hide any fear or insecurity about their relationship.

If he was going to be involved with Nic, he'd have to learn to read the emotions she was reluctant to show him. And that was something else that would be different from what he'd had with Heather, who had fervently believed in sharing all their feelings about everything.

But this wasn't the time to think about Heather.

"I don't think we made a mistake," he said firmly. "I still think it's been building between us for a long time. I do think I handled it badly. I got rattled. A little overwhelmed, I think. I needed a little time to process it all, so I took off. I'm sorry."

She studied his face for a moment and then smiled. "Apology accepted."

That was it? She didn't want explanations of why he'd felt overwhelmed? Of any conclusions he had reached since he'd left? She didn't want any promises that he wouldn't run out on her like that again?

She opened the box of treats he'd brought her. "Would you like one? The chocolate-dipped apricots are my favorite."

Still looking at her face, he accepted an apricot, which he ate in two bites. "You're right. That is good."

Nic set the box aside. "You've got a little chocolate on your mouth. Let me help you with it."

She leaned forward and covered his mouth with her own.

There were times when action was infinitely better than talking, he decided immediately, gathering her closer.

Chapter Thirteen

They never did get around to talking about why he'd panicked earlier. Joel didn't really want to talk about it yet, and Nic didn't seem to be any more eager to get into an in-depth examination of their feelings. It seemed easier all around to spend the remainder of the evening talking about inconsequential things, laughing, getting to know each other all over again as lovers rather than platonic friends.

He didn't spend the night. Neither of them was ready for that step. But it was quite late by the time he finally tore himself away from her, making her promise to call him if she needed anything at all.

He was back at her place the next evening after work, bringing take-out food with him. He wasn't sure if her radiant smile when she opened the door had more to do with her pleasure at seeing him or her relief at having someone to talk to.

She wasn't dealing with her enforced vacation well; she wanted to be back at work. Apparently she had spent much of the day on the phone with friends and coworkers, but that wasn't the same, she complained, as being out among them. By the time they'd finished dinner and dessert and had watched a couple of programs on TV, she was in better spirits, convinced that she should be able to return to work the next day.

"I don't think so," he said with a shake of his head. "You agreed to take the rest of the week to recover from that concussion. Your boss said he didn't want you back until you've been released by your doctor. You won't even get those stitches out for another few days. Why don't you just try to enjoy your time off and let yourself heal completely before you go back to work?"

She groaned and let her head fall back on the couch. "I'm so bored."

Smiling, he reached out to smooth the ragged edges of the tape that held her bandage on her chin. She'd been picking at it again, impatient with the feel of it against her skin. "You'll survive. You might even enjoy it if you gave yourself a chance."

"Right," she said, giving him an openly skeptical look. "Like you wouldn't be itching to get back to work by now."

She had him there. He'd be going crazy by now. But that didn't mean he was going to encourage her to go back to work sooner than she should. He had to admit that he was in no hurry to see her strap on her weapon again.

Again he stayed late, then made himself leave. Wearing a fuzzy robe and a sleepy smile, she saw him to the door without asking him to stay.

When his telephone rang early the next morning as he was getting ready to go to work, his first thought was that it was Nic. He was surprised when he heard his mother's voice on the other end of the line. "Mom? Is everything okay?"

"That's what I was going to ask you. I've tried calling you several times during the past couple of evenings and you never answered."

"You didn't leave a message."

"You know how I hate those machines."

He shook his head in exasperation. "Was there anything in particular you needed?"

"I wanted to ask about Nicole. How is she?"

"She's doing great. Impatient to get back to work."

Elaine made a tsking sound. "I can't imagine why. Did you hear about that police officer who was shot in Los Angeles yesterday? I read about it in the newspaper this morning."

Joel felt a muscle twitch in his jaw, but he kept his tone light. "Cabot is hardly Los Angeles, Mom. Nic's safe on the job here."

"She will never be safe as long as she wears a gun and apprehends lawbreakers. Anyone who becomes emotionally involved with her is going to have to learn to live with that somehow."

She couldn't have been more obvious if she'd slapped him upside the head. In response he said simply, "I'll tell her you asked about her. I'm sure she'll be pleased."

Sensing that he was preparing to disconnect, Elaine spoke more quickly. "Did Heidi call you?"

"No. Was she supposed to?"

"She said she might call to ask about Nic. And I think she wants to tell you about a young woman she'd like for you to meet. From what Heidi has said, she sounds ideal for you."

"Mother—"

"I'm not matchmaking, Joel. Heidi is."

Her logic failed to appease him. "I'm not interested in being the object of anyone's matchmaking. Especially Heidi's."

"She just wants you to be happy, Joel. She loves you."

"Tell her I love her, too. And I'm perfectly happy."

"But—"

"Mom, I'm sorry, but I have to go. I've got appointments this morning and I don't want to be late."

"Oh. Well, I guess we can talk later...."

"You bet," he said cheerfully, making a mental promise to be very busy for the foreseeable future. And then, because that made him feel guilty, he added, "Love you."

"I love you, too."

That was all he allowed her to say. He hung up quickly and reached for his car keys.

He felt a bit cowardly about practically hanging

up on his well-intentioned mother. He had deliberately avoided telling her that he and Nic had become
more than friends. And he could tell himself all he
wanted that it was only because the relationship was
too new and that he wasn't ready to share it with the
rest of the world yet, but he knew that wasn't the real
explanation.

The truth was, he knew his mother wouldn't
approve. Cowardly or not, he just didn't want to deal
with that now.

He looked at the photograph on his dresser. And
for once he had absolutely nothing to say.

"If you want me to do this, you're going to have
to lie still."

"Well, hurry up. Are you always this slow?"

"I'm not exactly working under optimal condi-
tions. If you'd have come to my office…"

"A pediatrician's office? I don't think so. What if
someone had seen me?"

"Afraid of ruining your tough-cop rep?"

"Heck, yes. I'd never live it down."

"Darn it, Nic, stop wiggling. You want me to snip
you instead of the stitches?"

"I should have just taken them out myself," she
muttered, forcing herself to be still. "I have
manicure scissors."

"If you'd have even tried that, I'd have made you
get new stitches."

She laughed at his ridiculous threat. "Oh, real
tough guy. I'm shaking."

Sitting beside her as she lay on her bed with her chin tilted toward him, Joel sighed. "Seriously, Nic, lie still, okay? I don't want to hurt you."

"Okay, I'll try. How many have you gotten out?"

He sighed. "One. We just started."

"Oh." Somewhat chastened, she dug her fingers into the bedspread beneath her to hide the apprehension she refused to allow him to see.

They'd already had an argument that morning about the stitches. Nic had asked him to remove them, since she wanted to report to work the next morning looking mostly healed from her freak accident. Joel had agreed that she'd healed well enough to remove the stitches, but he'd wanted to do it at his office, a suggestion she had vetoed.

"My brother took out his own stitches when he sliced his hand on a fish-gutting knife. He said it was no big deal and he sure wasn't going to pay a doctor to do it."

Joel hadn't been impressed by her argument, but he had reluctantly admitted that he could safely remove her stitches without going to the clinic. Now that she had nagged him into it, she was determined not to show him that it made her a little nervous.

She managed to remain still for the rest of the procedure, though she had to bite her tongue a couple of times when the slightly crusty stitches pulled as he removed them. To give him credit, he was amazingly gentle. She found that gazing up into his face helped take her mind off what he was doing.

He really did have a handsome face. She

wondered now why she'd ever thought of him as just an average, pleasant-looking guy.

He met her eyes for a moment and smiled, making his face even more appealing. "You're doing great now," he assured her. "Maybe you'll get a reward after all."

"I'm counting on it," she purred.

He cleared his throat. "Not a good idea to distract the doctor when he's holding scissors."

A few minutes later it was over. With a last swab of antibiotic over the mending wound, Joel pronounced it well on the way to being fully healed.

"It's actually a very dashing scar," he assured her with a smile. "Makes you look bold and adventurous."

She laughed. "That's always been my goal, of course."

"Of course."

She reached up to catch the collar of his shirt in both hands, drawing him down toward her. "I haven't thanked you yet for your expert care."

His mouth hovering just over hers, he replied, "It was entirely my pleasure."

"It will be," she promised and closed the gap between them.

It had been an amazing week, Nic thought as she lay against Joel's shoulder some time later. They had spent every evening together from the time Joel got home from work until he left late each night to walk next door.

They had talked as easily as they ever did, laughed as much as before, but with a new awareness now of the attraction simmering between them. They talked about their work, about the TV programs they watched together, about music and movies and sports. They talked about everything except their relationship. Or their past relationships. Or the future.

Okay, she thought with a wince, so maybe they had carefully avoided talking about the really important issues between them. That wasn't so bad, was it?

It was still early in their relationship. They didn't need to get all serious and introspective this soon.

He stirred and kissed the top of her head. "Are you hungry? I'm hungry."

It was only four in the afternoon, too early for dinner. "I have some snack stuff in the kitchen, I think."

"Sounds good. We can make a pot of coffee."

"Okay." She had noticed that Joel always seemed to find an excuse to get out of bed soon after they made love. Though he hadn't exactly run in panic since that first time, he wasn't one to cuddle and talk much afterward.

That seemed to be out of character to Nic. She'd have sworn he'd be the cuddle-and-talk type. Because she still wasn't convinced that he wasn't, she wondered if he worried about getting too serious in any conversations that might take place while they were still emotionally vulnerable.

They were going to have to really talk eventually, she mused as she slipped into her clothes. But she was in no more hurry than Joel to stray into that potentially dangerous territory.

They made coffee and put together a tray of cheeses, crackers and fruit. They carried the snacks into the living room and settled onto the couch with a pro football game playing on the television in front of them.

"Who's your pick?" Joel asked, nodding toward the screen. "Steelers or Packers?"

"Steelers."

"All right. I'll take the Packers. Five bucks."

"Sucker." She popped a grape in her mouth and leaned back into the couch cushions feeling quite content.

Stacking two types of cheese on a whole wheat cracker, Joel asked, "Have you heard from Aislinn lately? I haven't seen her around."

"She calls. She hasn't been around because she's been busy. She had two weddings, two birthdays and an anniversary party this weekend. They all wanted fairly elaborate cakes for the occasions."

"She's really talented at that, isn't she? Like an artist."

"She is an artist. Some of her cake designs have won awards. She could be working in a big-time restaurant setting, but she prefers staying here, making just enough money to live frugally but comfortably."

"Sounds like Ethan. He could be rich by now. He says he doesn't want to be rich. Doesn't want the hassles and headaches that go along with all that money."

"I sure didn't go into law enforcement for the money," she said with a laugh.

"That's not why I went into medicine, either."

"I know it's not. You love your work. Anyone can see that. Still, you do all right for yourself. You could be living fancier than you do. All the other doctors around here live over at the golf course."

He shrugged. "Why would I need a big house for just me? Maybe someday, but right now I'm perfectly happy where I am."

"I'm glad to hear that."

He munched on an apple slice, swallowed, then asked, "What about you? Won't your mother want her house back when she comes home?"

"She doesn't seem to be in any hurry to come back. She likes serving as Paul's hostess and taking care of him over there. But, yes, when she returns to Cabot, this is her home. I'm just watching over things for her. Which happens to be very convenient for me, since she won't take any rent money. It's letting me put some money away for a down payment on my own place someday."

"So you want to buy your own house eventually?" He kept his eyes on the television screen as he asked.

It was the closest they'd ever come to discussing the future. Telling herself he asked only to make idle conversation, she answered lightly, "Well, sure. Isn't that the American dream?"

"When do you think your mother will come home for good?"

"Probably in a couple of years. I talked to her this morning, by the way. She and Paul are coming here for Christmas. I can't wait to see them. They'll be here for almost a month, but then they're both planning to go back."

"Did you ever tell her what happened to you in Danston?"

"Well…sort of. I told her I took a fall and split my chin open, but I didn't see any need to give her all the details."

"Hmm."

She wasn't sure what she was supposed to read into that sound, but she hastily moved on. "Have you talked to your family lately?"

"Actually, yes. Ethan called this morning."

"Yeah? How's he doing?"

"It was kind of an odd call, actually. He asked me if I was aware that he'd never visited me here."

Nic cleared her throat. "Did he?"

"Mmm. I told him he was welcome to come anytime, of course. He said he might just do that in a couple of months."

"I think that's good. He should know what your life is like here."

"You didn't have anything to do with his sudden realization, did you?"

"I, um…"

"Nic?"

She sighed. "Okay, maybe I mentioned to him that I noticed none of your family has visited you here."

"Well, it's easier for me to go there than for all of them to come here," Joel said logically.

"Still, they seem to make a lot of assumptions about

your life without actually seeing it for themselves. Ethan didn't even know you paint watercolors."

Joel flushed. "I don't mention that to many people. I'm not all that good. It's just something I do to relax."

"I think you're very good," she said loyally. "That painting you did of the Old Mill in North Little Rock? It's really beautiful."

"You like that one?" He looked pleased.

"It's my favorite."

"Thank you."

She nodded. "You're welcome."

Her phone rang, and she answered it expecting to hear Aislinn on the other end. Instead it was one of her coworkers, one of the other female officers on the local force, making sure Nic would really be back at work the next day.

Carrying the phone into the kitchen so that Joel could watch the ball game undisturbed, Nic spent the next twenty minutes chatting, catching up on everything she'd missed during the past week and laughing at her friend's stories. By the time she hung up, she was even more eager than before to get back to work.

"Sorry," she said to Joel as she walked back into the living room. "That was Sandy, from work."

"No problem. I guess your coworkers are ready to have you back."

"As a matter of fact, they are."

"You'll be careful, won't you? I mean, you've just gotten over a concussion."

She smiled and patted his arm. "I'm always careful. You know that."

He gave her a look of disbelief. "Hence the six stitches I just pulled out of your chin."

Laughing, she wrapped her arms around his neck and leaned into him. "Are you worried about me, Brannon?"

He pulled her onto his lap, but his smile didn't quite reach his eyes. "Yes, I am."

"Don't be." She took a nip out of his ear and whispered, "I can take care of myself."

"I know," he said, but instead of sounding reassured, there was almost a hint of resignation in his voice.

Deciding not to pursue that topic any further at the moment, she pressed her lips to his. Joel seemed perfectly content to let conversation drop in favor of more pleasurable pursuits.

Chapter Fourteen

October slipped into November, and signs of the approaching holidays cropped up everywhere. It wasn't a particularly cold fall, and the weather was beautiful for the most part. Nic found herself walking around with a perpetual smile on her face, causing speculation among her coworkers.

When asked by a few particularly shrewd friends, she didn't deny that she was involved in a new relationship, though she didn't volunteer any information they didn't guess for themselves. She was resigned to being teased mercilessly when her coworkers found out she was dating a doctor, and that was exactly what she got when a couple of them learned the truth.

"Trying to marry money, eh, Sawyer?" one wise

guy jeered as they finished up a two-car call to a particularly ugly domestic dispute involving drunken cursing and wildly swinging fists and culminating with one of their perpetrators vomiting all over everyone around him. "Hoping he'll take you away from all this?"

Her nose still wrinkled in disgust, Nic handled the taunt with the ease of someone used to being the butt of jokes—and someone who also did a lot of the teasing. "Now why would I want to leave this life of glamour and nonstop adventure? Is there a better job in the world?"

Her fellow officer laughed and shook his head. "Not that I know of," he said, cheerfully swabbing at his pant leg with a grubby handkerchief.

While Nic didn't mind revealing that she was involved with Joel, she wasn't sure he was ready to go that public. If he'd told any of his local friends that he was seeing her, she didn't know about it.

They went out, of course. They had dinner, they saw movies, they attended a couple of parties. But Nic wondered if anyone who saw them together would realize that their yearlong friendship had recently changed.

Maybe Joel just wasn't the public-display-of-affection type. He was certainly demonstrative enough in private—though they had yet to talk about their feelings for each other.

She didn't know if he had told his family that they were now more than friends. She suspected that he had not. And she couldn't help wondering if he was simply waiting to see if their new relationship had a chance of lasting or if he didn't want to hear them express their disapproval. Didn't want to try to defend his choice to them.

She was under no illusions that her effort to rescue Heidi had made Joel's parents look at her differently. While they had expressed their gratitude on their friend's behalf, it was still obvious that they didn't see her as a fitting match for Joel.

She thought of her friends' teasing about her angling to marry money. She understood they didn't mean it. Anyone who knew her well had to be aware that she would never be motivated by something so shallow and ultimately unsatisfying. Of course, Joel's friends and family didn't know her very well, so maybe they had concerns about that.

But during the few moments she allowed herself to contemplate their resistance, the main reason she came up with was that she was so very different from Heather. She didn't want to believe that mattered so much, but she reluctantly acknowledged that the skeptics might have a point. If Joel had been so blissfully happy with Heather, why would he want to be involved now with someone who was almost diametrically opposite to his late wife?

But she wouldn't think of that now, she promised herself. After all, she and Joel were just enjoying the present, right? There had been no talk of a future together, and she wasn't looking for a long-term commitment anyway. Or so she told herself on an average of three times a day.

She didn't see much of Aislinn during those early weeks of November. Aislinn claimed to be very busy with her cake-decorating business, but Nic wondered if there was more to her friend's absence. Was she deliberately making herself scarce while Nic and Joel explored their new bond or was there something more to it? Was Aislinn seeing an ending that wasn't going to be happy?

Because she was determined not to spoil her present contentment by worrying about a future she couldn't completely control, Nic chose not to think any more about Aislinn's uncharacteristic behavior than she did about Joel's family's opinions. This would all work out or it wouldn't, she told herself prosaically. Either way, she could handle it. She'd survived broken relationships before, she could do so again.

Even as she made that brash vow to herself, she suspected that getting over Joel would be a lot harder than anything she had ever faced before.

Joel drew in a sharp breath as he parted Nic's calf-length terry-cloth robe and looked down at her right leg. "Damn it, Nic."

She chuckled, unchastened by his scolding. "It's just a scrape. It looks worse than it is. And you should see the other guy."

"You just recovered from all the bruises from your fall. Now your whole right calf is purple again—not to mention that nasty scrape."

"It's not as if I did it on purpose."

"You aren't supposed to tackle in flag football.

That's the whole point of the game. You know—so you won't be hurt?"

"I had to tackle him," she said with an unrepentant shrug and a grin. "He was going to score. And besides, he was taunting me. You wouldn't expect me to let him get away with that, would you? But if it makes you feel any better, I think he's going to have a black eye."

"Why would that make me feel better?" Joel demanded, looking at her in disbelief. "You could have been hurt, Nic. You both could have."

She sighed lustily. "Okay, so sometimes our flag football games get a little out of hand. I'll start trying to be more careful," she conceded unenthusiastically.

"Do that."

Having just returned from a medical meeting of some sort in Little Rock, Joel was still dressed in a dark jacket, a gray shirt and tie and charcoal slacks. He looked very much the successful young professional. He'd come straight to her place when he'd returned because he'd been held up by freeway traffic and was running late for the dinner date they'd planned.

He'd found Nic just getting out of the shower, having lost track of time herself when a group of off-duty coworkers had taken advantage of a beautiful Saturday afternoon to play in an area park. He'd caught a glimpse of her latest injuries when the robe had parted as she'd walked across the room toward him. And he hadn't stopped fussing since, she thought with a sigh.

"If we're going out to dinner, I'd better get

dressed," she said, grateful to change the subject. "You can run home and change if you want. We're not in any hurry."

He shrugged. "I'm okay. I'll just wear this."

Which meant she wouldn't be wearing the jeans and sweater she'd laid out on her bed, she thought, reluctantly putting them away. She could hardly wear jeans when Joel was dressed like Mr. *GQ*.

Pulling out her black slacks and black-and-purple sweater—the infamous Penderville Pirates outfit—she threw them on the bed and slipped out of her robe. "How was your meeting?"

His gaze was focused on her as he answered, and it would have been nice to think he was admiring the way she looked in her bra and panties. He probably did, but she was well aware that he was glaring at the deepening bruise on her right calf when he answered absently, "It was okay. Kind of dull."

"Sorry to hear that." She stepped into her pants, hiding the offending bruise from his sight, though she knew it was still in his mind.

Since they were dressed up, he drove her to a nice restaurant in North Little Rock, just over a twenty-minute drive away, where he encouraged her to order anything she wanted. "I'm having the steak and lobster tail," he informed her when she frowned at the prices listed on the right side of the menu. "You like seafood, don't you?"

She loved seafood, actually, but her budget rarely extended to these prices. Anything over ten bucks was an extravagance to her—and these meals were well over ten bucks.

"Look, they have Alaskan king crab legs," Joel pointed out helpfully. "I know you like those, I've heard you mention it to Aislinn."

"Well, yes, but…"

"That's settled, then. Want to split some stuffed mushrooms for an appetizer? If we're going to indulge tonight, we might as well go all out. Besides, I'm sure you worked off the calories today," he added in a mutter.

Putting the prices out of her mind, Nic set the menu aside. "I love stuffed mushrooms."

"Good. We might even save room for dessert. The key lime pie here is the best I've had in this state."

Nic could almost hear the echo of her co-workers' teasing in her mind as she listened to Joel rattle off their food order without seeming to even care that the tab was going to be higher than her monthly electric bill. And it wasn't even a special occasion, she mused, reaching for her water glass. Just dinner.

She told herself that Joel wasn't trying to impress her. He had been in the mood for surf and turf and he could afford it, so why not treat himself—and her—if he wanted?

Their conversation was just a bit more stilted than usual, maybe because of the atypical formality of their surroundings. They talked about his meeting, and about her game with her friends—though that seemed to be a rather sticky subject, for some reason.

Finally they just concentrated on their meals, agreeing occasionally that the food was delicious.

It wasn't late when they returned home, so Nic invited Joel inside. It occurred to her as he entered that they never went to his house. She wondered if there was any significance to that or if it was just coincidence. She seemed to be trying to read too much into everything tonight, she told herself with an impatient shake of her head.

She assured herself that she wasn't being cowardly when she wrapped her arms around Joel's neck and smiled flirtatiously up at him. She wasn't really avoiding any further awkward conversation. She just missed touching him.

"That," she told him, "was a truly delicious meal. A real treat. I owe you a special dinner in return. Maybe I'll cook my famous shrimp-and-asparagus casserole for you soon."

He looped his arms loosely around her waist. "Famous, huh?"

"I've taken it to two department potlucks and gotten rave reviews both times."

"Then I'll definitely have to try it."

"In the meantime..." She rose on tiptoes to brush her lips against his.

"Oh, yeah. In the meantime..." He gathered her close.

They moved to her bedroom, and the nice clothes were thrown in a careless heap on the carpeting. Mouths fused, hands roaming, they rolled on the bed, heat building rapidly between them.

Nic flinched instinctively when Joel's shin scraped over her freshly bruised calf. He stilled immediately, making her silently curse herself for revealing her momentary discomfort.

"Did I hurt you?"

"No," she assured him, tugging at his shoulders. "I'm fine."

He held back with a frown. "Just let me look at your leg…."

"Later," she said, pulling him down to her. "I'm busy right now."

"Nic—"

But her name was smothered against her lips. After a moment, Joel stopped resisting.

They were sitting in front of Nic's TV a few nights later when they almost got into another quarrel. It started innocently enough. They were watching a newsmagazine-style show and they were both intrigued by a story about a program for at-risk youth that had been initiated by a psychologist and a police officer in Baltimore. Because both Joel and Nic had professional interests in troubled kids, the program sparked a discussion between them about whether a modified version would be helpful in their small town.

"You could do something like that," Joel suggested as if the idea had just occurred to him. "Work with at-risk kids, I mean."

"I do, sort of," she reminded him. "A lot of my calls involve kids in trouble."

He shook his head. "I didn't mean in the course

of your regular police work. I meant you should think about focusing exclusively on that work. You'd be good at it. Maybe in a high school setting. You know, like a counselor."

"A counselor?" Nic stiffened and pulled slightly away from him on the couch. "I'm a cop, Joel. Not a shrink."

"But you said you wanted to work with kids—"

"I'd be interested in getting involved in a program like the one we just heard about. A joint thing with the police department and social services. I never said I wanted to leave the force."

"Look, I didn't mean anything by it," he said getting a good look at her expression. "We were just talking."

Nodding, she pushed herself off the couch. "I think I'll get a soda. You want anything?"

"No, I'm fine. Nic—"

"I'll be right back," she said and escaped into the kitchen. She needed a couple of minutes to compose herself before she rejoined him.

Maybe she was reading too much into things again, but she had been badly shaken when Joel had seemed to be pushing her into the same career his late wife had once pursued. Surely he hadn't meant it that way. It probably had just been a spur-of-the-moment comment made in response to something he'd thought she said. But telling herself that didn't ease the sick feeling deep inside her stomach.

At his office, Joel had just finished caring for a child with a painful ear infection and was spending a few minutes returning telephone calls, before moving toward an exam room for the next appointment.

"Hey, Joel," his partner, Bob McCafferty, called from down the hallway. "Did you hear the news?"

"No, what news?"

"There was a hostage situation over by the tracks this morning. Some meth-head holed up with his ex-girlfriend and her kid. Threatened to kill himself and take them with him—and a few cops to boot. I heard your neighbor was right in the middle of it all."

Joel literally felt his heart skip a beat. "Nic?" he managed to say coherently, his hand clenching around the chart he held. "Is she…?"

Bob held up a hand and shook his head. "Chill. She's okay. From what I heard, no one was hurt. It got hairy for a while, but it all ended okay."

The breath left Joel's lungs in a rush that left him a little dizzy. "That's…good to hear."

"Big excitement for this town, huh? I bet your neighbor will have a good story to share with you later."

"Yeah. I'll have to be sure and ask her about it," Joel said grimly. "Excuse me, Bob, I've got a patient waiting."

He needed to stay very busy for the rest of the day, he told himself. Too busy to think about what might have happened.

As he pasted on a professional smile and pushed open the door to the examining room, he could almost hear the echo of his mother's voice reminding him that anyone who cared about a police officer would have to learn to live with daily fear.

It was time for him to do some very serious thinking about his relationship with Officer Nicole Sawyer.

"I don't think I can handle this, Nic."

A sick feeling inside her, Nic stared at the man who faced her from a few feet away in her living room, his expression stark. This scene was becoming all too familiar, she realized on a wave of sadness. She knew exactly what was coming next.

"Let me guess," she said unsteadily. "It's not me. It's you."

Looking miserable, Joel shoved his hands into the pockets of his dark slacks. "I think you're being sarcastic, but you're right. It isn't you. I'm the one who has a problem with your work."

"This might make sense to me if I was on the job in New York or L.A. Hell, even Little Rock," she added bitterly. "But here? Sorry, Joel, this sounds like a pretty feeble excuse to break it off."

"It isn't an excuse. It's an explanation."

"Look, if you're tired of being together, just say so, okay? We never said this was a long-term thing. We were just having some fun together. If it isn't fun for you anymore, then fine. It's over. No hard feelings."

Just a broken heart she would never let him see, she promised herself, her chin high, her eyes dry—and they would remain that way, at least until she was alone.

He scowled. "You haven't heard anything I've said, have you? It wasn't just a good time for me. It was real. Too damned real."

She wasn't sure she believed him. Maybe because

it would hurt too badly to think he had really fallen for her but still didn't truly understand her. "Yeah, okay. It was real. And now it's over. Because I'd rather be a police officer than to become something else you would choose for me."

"Because you're reckless," he shot back at her, looking almost angry now. "Because you take chances you don't have to take. Because you're the first one to jump into the middle of a fight. The one who breaks the rules even if it means you could get hurt. I can't spend every day worrying that the next time, you'll go too far. I care about you far too much for that. But you won't even consider making a few changes to keep yourself safe."

"I won't try to turn myself into someone I'm not just to make it easier for you to be with me," she said fiercely. "This is who I am, Joel. I'm not a saint. I don't have an advanced degree. I don't want to be a counselor. I'm a cop. As much as I care about you, I can't change for you. It just wouldn't work."

Her veiled references to Heather had made Joel's eyes darken and his mouth thin to a hard slit. "I haven't asked you to be anyone but yourself," he growled. "All I've ever wanted is for you to be careful. I don't think that's too much to ask."

She twisted her hands in front of her. "Did you ever tell your mother we were dating? Or Ethan?"

He blinked, disconcerted by the apparent non sequitur. "I don't—"

"Did you?"

He shook his head. "No."

"Why not?"

"I—" He paused, then shrugged. "I guess I was waiting for the right time."

"But you never really thought that time would come, did you? You didn't think it would last long enough for you to have to tell them. And you didn't want to have to admit to them that they were right when they told you I was all wrong for you."

"I didn't—"

"The fact is, you never argued when everyone told you how wrong I was for you because you agreed with them. And you know why I'm all wrong, Joel? Because I'm not Heather! You could try all you want to turn me into her, but it would never work, as I guess you've finally figured out for yourself."

Several shades of color drained from his face. She might have felt guilty about it, but the more she thought about him dumping her just because she'd performed her job that day, the angrier she became.

"That was incredibly unfair. I never compared you to Heather."

"Didn't you?" She stalked to the door and opened it. "You know what, Joel? You're right. It *isn't* me. It's you. And I think you'd better leave now."

"Nic—"

"Please go."

He sighed. "If that's what you want. I'll call you later."

"Don't bother. I'll be busy." Okay, so maybe she was being churlish. She was mad.

He left without another word. Just walked out, taking her heart with him.

Nic thought about bursting into tears, but she was too angry even for that. She paced instead, muttering beneath her breath.

When the doorbell rang twenty minutes later, she almost didn't answer it. If it was Joel, she didn't want to talk to him. And she wasn't in the mood to visit with anyone else. Except Aislinn maybe. And because suddenly she knew who was calling, she opened the door.

Aislinn took one look at Nic's face and closed the door behind her. "It must have been bad."

"He dumped me," Nic said, forcing the words out between clenched teeth. "Joel dumped me."

"Nic, I'm so sorry—"

Nic swallowed hard, holding up a hand to stop Aislinn's expression of sympathy. "Can you believe he had the nerve to give me The Speech?"

Her friend grimaced. "Not—"

"Yeah, that one. The it's-not-you-it's-me spiel. The jerk."

Aislinn walked into the kitchen, reached into the refrigerator and pulled out a bottle of wine. "Tell me from the beginning," she said, opening the cabinet where Nic stored the wineglasses.

Nic was already digging in the freezer for ice cream. "He started yelling at me pretty much the minute I opened the door to him. For doing my job this morning—can you believe that?"

"The hostage situation? I heard about it. Everyone was talking about it."

Nic shook her head impatiently. "Everyone was probably exaggerating. It wasn't that big a deal. The guy was all talk. He never even took a shot at us."

"Joel didn't find any comfort in that?" Aislinn asked, pouring generous servings of wine.

An enormous scoop of ice cream plopped into a bowl. "He wasn't interested in hearing it. Can you believe he actually asked if I would consider quitting my job?"

Aislinn winced. "Surely not."

"He said he didn't think he could ever get used to my work. The way he phrased it made me think he was hoping I would volunteer to quit if it made him happy."

"Maybe you misunderstood."

Nic slid a bowl across the table to Aislinn and stabbed a spoon into her own mound of toffee-chip. "Trust me, I didn't misunderstand. He called me reckless. He said he wished I were more like Heather."

Aislinn set down her spoon with a clatter. "He didn't say that."

Nic flushed. "Okay, he didn't say those words exactly. But he told me the other night that I should become a counselor for at-risk kids. I told you Heather was a family counselor. Do you really think that's simply a coincidence?"

"It does sound bad," Aislinn admitted.

"I can't let Joel turn me into a pale copy of his late wife."

"You really think that's what he's trying to do?"

Nic pushed aside her barely touched bowl of ice cream and reached for her wine. "It's the only way I'd be an acceptable match for him. To his friends and family. Even to him."

"Oh, Nic—"

The sympathy in Aislinn's voice broke through some of the anger that had been protecting Nic from the pain. She swallowed hard against a sudden thick lump in her throat. "It was a mistake from the beginning."

"You fell in love with him, didn't you?"

Nic set down her wine untasted. With anyone else, she would have given an immediate vehement denial. Because it was Aislinn, she said, "I'll get over it."

"You don't think there's a chance…?"

"He dumped me," she reminded her. "He said he couldn't accept what—and who—I am. Does that sound like there's a chance?"

"Not really, no," Aislinn admitted sadly.

Even though she'd said it herself, it hurt to hear Aislinn confirm it.

"You had a feeling this wasn't going to work out well, didn't you?"

Aislinn made patterns in her ice cream with her spoon. "I had a feeling you were going to be hurt," she admitted. "I did try to warn you."

"I know. And I didn't listen. I thought it would be worth it."

Looking at her intently, Aislinn asked, "And was it?"

Nic rolled her glass between her hands, giving

the question some thought. The last few weeks had been so special that she could hardly look back at them now without tears. Would she eventually be able to think of them with pleasure, treasuring the moments she and Joel had spent together, savoring the memories of lazy evenings and passionate interludes?

"I don't know yet."

"Give it time. And whenever you need to talk, you know I'm here."

Nic nodded.

"There's just one more thing I need to say, and then we'll change the subject for now, okay?"

"What is it?"

Aislinn reached out to lay her hand on Nic's arm, a warm, supportive gesture. "It really isn't you, Nic. There's nothing at all wrong with you. You don't have to compare yourself to anyone."

Tears threatened then, but Nic blinked them back. "Thanks. You could be a little biased."

"Hell, yes. But I'm still right."

Managing a weak smile, Nic reached for her ice cream again. "Well, of course you are. You're always right."

Aislinn's answering smile was strained. "There are times when I wish I were wrong."

He didn't really want to, but Joel went home for Thanksgiving. He might have made excuses to stay away that year, claiming to be too busy with work, but it seemed so important to his mother for him to come. Besides, his father had been ill—nothing too serious, just an upper-respiratory infection—and Joel would have felt too guilty to skip out on them, even though he'd been home only a few weeks before for the reunion.

He regretted his decision almost immediately. The memories that haunted him here now were ones of Nic. Every time he passed the guest room, he half expected to see her in the doorway. Each time one of his parents said something that amused him, he found himself looking for her to share a secret smile.

He noticed that he had begun to walk down the upstairs hallway without looking at the walls. For the first time all those old pictures bugged him. He hadn't realized how much his family was stuck in the past. What was keeping them from moving on? Was it partially his fault?

Maybe it was past time he put away a few photographs of his own.

Having arrived late Wednesday afternoon, he would be leaving early Saturday morning. He stayed close to his parents' house during his visit, not particularly anxious to run into any of his old classmates again so soon.

His mother waited until Friday afternoon to broach the subject of Nic. Everyone had asked about her as soon as he'd arrived, of course, but after he'd assured them she was fully recovered from her fall, they hadn't mentioned her again.

"Have you seen Nicole much lately?" Elaine asked as she and Joel worked on a jigsaw puzzle together at a table in one corner of the den. It was one of her favorite hobbies, and she often drafted her husband or one of her sons into helping her, mostly just to keep her company.

"Not really," he said, keeping his gaze focused on the jumble of puzzle pieces. "We've both been busy. It's been a couple of weeks since we talked."

He didn't add that he, for one, had been very careful to avoid running into Nic, and he was sure she had done the same thing. Considering they lived only a few yards apart, it was odd how few fleeting glimpses he'd had of her since their breakup two weeks earlier.

"So she hasn't had any dangerous escapades lately?"

Joel scowled down at the puzzle piece in his hand. It really should fit into the section in front of him, but he couldn't seem to find a place for it. "She's a police officer, Mom. What you and I might consider dangerous escapades are just a typical part of her work week."

The bitterness he heard in his own voice made him grimace. So maybe he was exaggerating just a little. As Nic herself had pointed out, it wasn't as if she worked a SWAT team in a teeming metropolis. But the fact was, she did respond to dangerous domestic-disturbance calls. And she did confront the occasional violent addict or aggressive drunk.

She spent a great deal of her time dealing with people who broke the law and were resistant to the idea of being punished for doing so. She wore a sidearm as casually as some women donned pearls. Downplay it all she wanted, her job was a dangerous one.

Elaine shook her head in disapproval. "I don't know how her mother deals with the worry. It must be so difficult for her."

"I don't know. I've only met her mother once, soon after I moved in next door. But she seemed to have come to terms with Nic's job."

Nic had told him that her mother had initially been resistant to the idea of her daughter joining the police force, but she'd come around because she wanted Nic to pursue a career she loved and in which she could make a difference. He wondered why Nic's family hadn't tried harder to convince her that there were many other jobs that could provide her with that same satisfaction.

Elaine slipped a puzzle piece into place. "I have a little confession to make," she said without looking up. "I worried for a while that you and Nicole were romantically involved."

"We aren't," Joel said shortly, still trying to find a match for the piece he held.

"Good. She's a very nice young woman, but I just don't think she's right for you."

He glanced up at her from across the game table, trying to think of a response to that. And then he looked back down at the puzzle, unable to quite meet his mother's eyes. "Maybe it's the other way around, Mom. Maybe I'm not right for her."

Elaine shook her head, sounding confused when she said, "I don't really see the difference."

"I know you don't. But I do."

For some reason, he was able at that moment to

fit the puzzle piece he held into its position. He snapped it into place with more force than was absolutely necessary.

And then he drew a deep breath and looked back up at his mother. "I think we need to talk about your photo gallery upstairs."

Nic was tired. She didn't know why she was so weary. She'd slept well enough the night before, and nothing particularly eventful had occurred that day. She was well aware that the exhaustion was more emotional than physical.

Maybe it was because the days were getting so very short, and it seemed to be dark more than it was light these days. But even as that thought crossed her mind, she knew it wasn't the real reason. This wasn't general seasonal depression. It had a very specific cause.

She would get past this, she promised herself. She'd been hurt, true, but her heart would heal, just as her body had done after her fall. Maybe it would take a little longer this time. Maybe it would take a *lot* longer. But she'd be okay. She always was.

She opened her refrigerator. She wasn't particularly hungry, but she would eat. She wasn't going to be one of those scorned women who sat around moping and wasting away, letting her health deteriorate. She wouldn't let anyone do that to her, not even the only man she'd ever allowed to steal her heart.

When she heard Joel's tap on the back door, her first, uncharacteristically cowardly instinct was to pretend she wasn't home. It was pride more than the knowledge that he surely knew she was there that made her draw a deep breath, square her shoulders and open the door.

He looked like hell. Matt Damon after a weeklong bender maybe, she thought irrelevantly—even if Aislinn didn't see the resemblance.

Maybe she had been sleeping okay, but Joel obviously had not. And even as her heart clenched, she knew she couldn't allow herself to be influenced by his obvious misery—not if it meant she had to sacrifice who she was in order to try and make him happy again.

"What do you want, Joel?" she asked, keeping her voice toneless to hide the emotions that had welled in her at the sight of him.

"There's something I need to say to you."

She hoped he hadn't come to ask if they could still be friends. As much as she missed the easy friendship they'd had before their disastrous attempt at being more, she really didn't think they could get it back now. It would be too painful—at least for her. She wished it could be different, but she knew herself too well to believe she could pretend he hadn't broken her heart.

"What is it?"

"May I come in?"

She hesitated only a moment before stepping out of the doorway. Looking faintly relieved, Joel entered the kitchen and closed the door behind him.

Nic shoved her hands into the pockets of the flannel dorm pants she'd changed into along with a long-sleeve fleece top after arriving home from work half an hour earlier. She didn't offer him anything to drink, didn't even offer him a seat. She wanted this to be over quickly.

"Well?" she prodded when he didn't immediately speak but stood silently in front of her, one hand squeezing the back of his neck.

Joel sighed. "I'm not sure how to start. First, I want to apologize. I hurt you, and that was never my intention."

"Apology accepted. Thanks for coming by." She reached for the door.

He shook his head, looking almost amused. "You really don't believe in making things easier, do you? I'm not leaving yet. Not until I've had my say."

"I think you said all you needed to say last time you were here."

He shook his head again. "That wasn't all by a long shot. I left a few things out."

"Such as—?

"Such as the fact that I love you. That I've loved you for quite some time."

Nic flinched. She tried to hide the reaction by turning away. "Please don't."

"Not saying it won't make it go away, Nic. I love you. I fell in love with you even when I was convinced that I was all wrong for you."

"Don't you have that the wrong way around?" she couldn't help asking with a tinge of bitterness. "Don't you mean that I'm all wrong for you?"

"No," he answered firmly. "That isn't what I

mean at all. I knew I would be damned lucky if you would have me. I just didn't think I had what it took to hold you."

She turned back to frown at him. "I don't know what you mean."

He raised a hand, palm upward, as if trying to grasp the right words from the air. "You date rodeo cowboys. You hang out with cops. People who don't think twice about risking their lives in the line of duty. Your best friend is probably a certifiable psychic, despite her denials."

"And you hang out with doctors and lawyers and professors and you date psychologists and beauty queens," she shot back. "We're from different circles. Isn't that what you were trying to tell me before?"

He shook his head, looking frustrated. "You seem to believe I think of you as somehow inferior to the other people I know. You couldn't be more wrong. I just couldn't see you being interested in someone so completely ordinary for long. So damned cowardly."

Though he'd shaken her, she clung to her skepticism. "I know why you wanted me to quit the force. To go back to college. You wanted me to be more like you. Like…"

She found she couldn't say Heather's name just then. But she knew he was aware of exactly who he meant.

"That's exactly why I wanted you to quit. Oh, not to make you more like me—or anyone else," he added. "But because of my own cowardice. I was afraid for you, Nic. Afraid of losing you. I'd lost someone once. I didn't think I had the strength to go through it again."

"Joel—"

He shook his head with a wry smile. "As far as I was concerned, that very fear made me all wrong for you. I doubt that the other guys you've dated spent all their time worrying about you."

"Anyone who gets involved with a cop spends a great deal of time worrying," she replied. "It's part of the job and it's the reason a lot of their relationships don't work out. I don't think of you as a coward because you were worried, but I can't change who I am."

"I've come to realize during the past few weeks that I don't want you to change. Why would I? I fell in love with you exactly as you are."

He had said it again. And it scared her just as much to hear it this time. He thought *he* was a coward? He had no idea how hard she was shaking inside now, so afraid that she was misunderstanding what he seemed to be telling her. "Everyone thinks I'm wrong for you. Your family. Your friends. They think you should find someone more like Heather."

She'd found the strength to say the name this time. She'd had to, since she still felt as though the memory of Joel's late wife was standing between them.

"My family and friends don't know you well enough to know whether we're right for each other or not. They'll learn to love you once I tell them how much you mean to me. All they really want is for me to be happy, Nic. That doesn't mean they know best how to accomplish that."

"And you think you do know?"

"Yes." He smiled at her then, though his eyes were very serious. "Being with you will make me happy."

She swallowed hard. "It didn't before," she reminded him miserably.

"That was my fault, not yours. You're right, I was trying too hard to ease my fears by trying to control circumstances that were out of my hands. But I've done a lot of thinking while we've been apart. And I've realized we aren't so very different after all."

She frowned. "We aren't?"

"No. Your job involves saving lives. So does mine. Maybe no one's shooting at me while I work, but— you know what?—it takes a hell of a lot of courage to be a physician. Parents literally put the lives of their precious children in my hands, and I accept that responsibility even though I live in dread of making a mistake or missing something that could have dire consequences for my patients."

"Of course it takes courage. I've told you dozens of times that I don't know how you do it."

"I do it because I love my work. It defines who I am. I wouldn't let anyone talk me into doing anything else. I think you understand that better than anyone else I know."

"I do understand that."

He nodded, his eyes growing a little warmer. "I know you do. And there are a lot more things we have in common. We both value our families. We've known what it's like to lose someone we love. Neither of us give a flip about climbing social ladders or trying to impress anyone by wearing the right clothes or driving the right car or living in the right neighborhood. That isn't what motivates us. It isn't how we define success."

"No," she admitted. "I've never cared about stuff like that."

"Neither have I. It was one of the things that exasperated Heather most about me," he added conversationally. "Not that she was a snob or anything, but she liked being in the top social circles. She wanted me to pursue the best residencies and appointments.

"She'd hoped that I'd be named chief of staff of some prestigious hospital, which was never a serious goal of mine. She wouldn't have been content to settle here, living in a modest house while I worked as a partner in a small-town pediatric clinic. She would have considered it her duty to push me into more, for what she considered my own best interests."

Nic was startled by his revelation. She couldn't see him ever being happy in some big, fiercely competitive, social-climbing setting. Had Heather really thought he would like that? Or had he changed so much during the past few years?

"Don't get me wrong, Heather had a heart as big as the sky. She was an excellent therapist who cared a great deal about her clients. But she liked the good life and had a weakness for expensive clothes and jewelry. She'd have reveled in an exclusive country-club environment—and I'd have gone along to make her happy. But I'm happy here with my small clinic and my regular patients."

"I can't imagine you being anywhere else."

He smiled. "That's because you've come to know me very well, Nic. You wouldn't try to change me—which makes what I tried to do to you even less forgivable."

"I didn't think I could compete with Heather's memory," she whispered.

"You never have to try. I loved Heather, but she wasn't perfect. I don't think she would want me to put her memory on some untouchable pedestal. That would make her less than she really was—a bright, special, unique woman with very human strengths and weaknesses."

Nic bit her lower lip, unsure what to say next.

Joel took a step closer to her. "I spent some time recently looking at those pictures in my mother's hallway. And I realized that too many people, including me, maybe, had gotten into the habit of thinking my whole life was captured in those photographs. They haven't taken into account all the things I've accomplished during the past five and a half years since Heather died. Finishing my residency, starting the clinic, buying a house, making new friends. Building a new life for myself.

"I don't want to spend the rest of my life alone with old memories, Nic. And I'm not looking to recreate what I once had. I'm ready for a new start. A new future. And I'd like to build that future with you, if I haven't destroyed all chance of that by being such a jerk. Have I?"

"I'm not going to quit my job," she warned, still

half-afraid to hope. "I'll work toward promotions and new assignments because I've always had ambitions in my field, but I will perform my duties as they occur, even if that occasionally puts me at risk."

He might have paled just a little, but he nodded. "I can live with that. I'm not saying I'll ever stop worrying about you, but I can deal with my fears as long as I know you're taking reasonable precautions."

"I don't have a death wish, Joel. I'm not as reckless as you've implied. But maybe I've taken a little less care than I should have in the past. As long as it doesn't interfere with my work, I'll try to be a little more cautious in the future. Maybe I'll stop tackling in flag football."

"That's a start," he said with a smile. "Does this mean you're willing to give it another try?"

"I'm not sure I have much choice," she answered quietly. "I'm in love with you, too."

"Nic—"

He reached for her, but she evaded him, holding up one unsteady hand. "You hurt me," she said sternly, giving him a warning glare. "If you do it again, I'll kick your butt all the way back to Birmingham."

Joel laughed and tugged her into his arms. "I believe you. And if I ever find out that you've risked your life unnecessarily, I'll kick yours to Tulsa."

She wrapped her arms around his neck, beginning to smile for the first time since she had opened the door to him. "All of a sudden you're a tough guy, huh?"

He grinned down at her. "I guess you're corrupting me."

She grew serious again for a moment. She had a few more admissions to make. "It wasn't all your fault, Joel. I didn't fight hard enough for us. I accused you of being resigned to failure, when the truth was that I never expected us to last. I let myself be too influenced by other people's opinions. Maybe I started to believe that I wasn't good enough for you. That I couldn't measure up. And you weren't the only one who was a coward. I was afraid to show you how much I cared. How much I wanted to make it work between us. I won't let that happen again."

"We both made mistakes, Nic. Since neither of us is perfect, I'm sure we'll make more. But we'll get it right this time. It turns out we're both willing to fight for what we want when it matters this much."

She still found it hard to believe that Joel had worried that he wasn't good enough for her. That it was he who didn't measure up. Maybe it would take a while for both of them to be reassured that they could really make this work. But she was willing to give it all the time they needed, she thought, lifting her mouth to Joel's. As long as they loved each other, she couldn't imagine any obstacle they couldn't overcome.

They had both lived through some dark days in their lives, she thought, closing her eyes and losing herself in his embrace. But she predicted sunny days ahead.

Joel loved her and she loved him. What more could she possibly ask?

Epilogue

The telephone rang a few hours later, and Nic reached over Joel's tired, sated body to pick up the bedside extension. "Hello?"

"Hi," Aislinn said. "How's it going?"

The smile in her friend's voice made Nic suspect that Aislinn knew exactly how things were going, but she answered anyway. "Joel and I are back together."

He smiled lazily up at her and reached up to touch her face, his hazel eyes glowing with physical satisfaction and a pure inner peace that she had never seen there before. Feeling exactly the same way, she smiled back at him.

"I'm very happy to hear that," Aislinn said. "I'll let you get back to…whatever you were doing."

"What? No predictions?" Nic asked, only half teasing.

Aislinn's voice was warm with affection when she replied, "I have a feeling it's going to work this time. If I really were a psychic, I'm sure I would predict a lifetime of happiness for the two of you."

Nic swallowed a lump in her throat. "Thanks, Aislinn. I'll see you tomorrow, okay?"

She hung up the phone, then nestled her cheek into Joel's shoulder. "Aislinn predicts a bright future for us."

"I'm glad to hear that. But your friend still makes me a little nervous, Nic."

She chuckled. "She would be amused to hear that. I wonder how she and Ethan would feel about each other?"

Joel laughed. "Oh, man, you're really crazy if you think you could pull off that match. Let's just concentrate on our own relationship and let Aislinn and Ethan find their own destinies, shall we?"

"You're probably right. It was just a thought."

Joel's hands slid slowly down her bare back, restoking embers that she thought they'd already extinguished for one evening. "I have a few thoughts of my own," he murmured. "I love you, Nic."

Forgetting about Aislinn and Ethan—and anyone else except this man she loved with her whole heart—Nic covered Joel's mouth in a joyous, eager kiss.

* * * * *

"Now that's the kind of man you should be looking for," my mother, the self-appointed keeper of my shelf-life stamp, says. She points with her fork at a man in the corner of The Steak-Out Restaurant, a dive I've just been hired to redecorate. Making this restaurant look four-star will be hard, but not half as hard as getting through lunch without strangling the woman across the table from me. "*He* would make a good husband."

"Oh, you can tell that from across the room?" I

ask, wondering how it is she can forget that when we had trouble getting rid of my last husband, she shot him. "Besides being ten minutes away from death if he actually eats all that steak, he's twenty years too old for me and—shallow woman that I am—twenty pounds too heavy. Besides, I am *so* not looking for another husband here. I'm looking to design a new image for this place, looking for some sense of ambience, some feeling, something I can build a proposal on for them."

My mother studies the man in the corner, tilting her head, the better to gauge his age, I suppose. I think she's grimacing, but with all the Botox and Restylane injected into that face, it's hard to tell. She takes another bite of her steak salad, chews slowly so that I don't miss the fact that the steak is a poor cut and tougher than it should be. "You're concentrating on the wrong kind of proposal," she says finally. "Just look at this place, Teddi. It's a dive. There are hardly any other diners. What does *that* tell you about the food?"

"That they cater to a dinner crowd and it's lunch-time," I tell her.

I don't know what I was thinking bringing her here with me. I suppose I thought it would be better than eating alone. There really are days when my common sense goes on vacation. Clearly, this is one of them. I mean, really, did I not resolve less than three weeks ago that I would not let my mother get to me anymore?

What good are New Year's resolutions, anyway?

Mario approaches the man's table and my mother

studies him while they converse. Eventually Mario leaves the table with a huff, after which the diner glances up and meets my mother's gaze. I think she's smiling at him. That or she's got indigestion. They size each other up.

I concentrate on making sketches in my notebook and try to ignore the fact that my mother is flirting. At nearly seventy, she's developed an unhealthy interest in members of the opposite sex to whom she isn't married.

According to my father, who has broken the TMI rule and given me Too Much Information, she has no interest in sex with him. Better, I suppose, to be clued in on what they aren't doing in the bedroom than have to hear what they might be doing.

"He's not so old," my mother says, noticing that I have barely touched the Chinese chicken salad she warned me not to get. "He's got about as many years on you as you have on your little cop friend."

She does this to make me crazy. I know it, but it works all the same. "Drew Scoones is not my little 'friend.' He's a detective with whom I—"

"Screwed around," my mother says. I must look shocked, because my mother laughs at me and asks if I think she doesn't know the "lingo."

What I thought she didn't know was that Drew and I actually tangled in the sheets. And, since it's possible she's just fishing, I sidestep the issue and tell her that Drew is just a couple of years younger than me and that I don't need reminding. I dig into my salad with renewed vigor, determined to show my mother that Chinese chicken salad in a steak place was not the stupid choice it's proving to be.

After a few more minutes of my picking at the wilted leaves on my plate, the man my mother has me nearly engaged to pays his bill and heads past us toward the back of the restaurant. I watch my mother take in his shoes, his suit and the diamond pinkie ring that seems to be cutting off the circulation in his little finger.

"Such nice hands," she says after the man is out of sight. "Manicured." She and I both stare at my hands. I have two popped acrylics that are being held on at weird angles by bandages. My cuticles are ragged and there's marker decorating my right hand from measuring carelessly when I did a drawing for a customer.

Twenty minutes later she's disappointed that he managed to leave the restaurant without our noticing. He will join the list of the ones I let get away. I will hear about him twenty years from now when—according to my mother—my children will be grown and I will still be single, living pathetically alone with several dogs and cats.

After my ex, that sounds good to me.

The waitress tells us that our meal has been taken care of by the management and, after thanking Mario, the owner, complimenting him on the wonderful meal and assuring him that once I have redecorated his place people will be flocking here in droves (I actually use those words and ignore my mother when she rolls her eyes), my mother and I head for the restroom.

My father—unfortunately not with us today—has the patience of a saint. He got it over the years of living with my mother. She, perhaps as a result, figures he has the patience for both of them, and feels justified having none. For her, no rules apply, and a little thing like a picture of a man on the door to a public restroom is certainly no barrier to using the john. In all fairness, it does seem silly to stand and wait for the ladies' room if no one is using the men's room.

Still, it's the idea that rules don't apply to her, signs don't apply to her, conventions don't apply to her. She knocks on the door to the men's room. When no one answers she gestures to me to go in ahead. I tell her that I can certainly wait for the ladies' room to be free and she shrugs and goes in herself.

Not a minute later there is a bloodcurdling scream from behind the men's room door.

"Mom!" I yell. "Are you all right?"

Mario comes running over, the waitress on his heels. Two customers head our way while my mother continues to scream.

I try the door, but it is locked. I yell for her to open it and she fumbles with the knob. When she finally manages to unlock and open it, she is white behind her two streaks of blush, but she is on her feet and appears shaken but not stirred.

"What happened?" I ask her. So do Mario and the waitress and the few customers who have migrated to the back of the place.

She points toward the bathroom and I go in,

thinking it serves her right for using the men's room. But I see nothing amiss.

She gestures toward the stall, and, like any self-respecting and suspicious woman, I poke the door open with one finger, expecting the worst.

What I find is worse than the worst.

The husband my mother picked out for me is sitting on the toilet. His pants are puddled around his ankles, his hands are hanging at his sides. Pinned to his chest is some sort of Health Department certificate.

Oh, and there is a large, round, bloodless bullet hole between his eyes.

Four Nassau County police officers are securing the area, waiting for the detectives and crime scene personnel to show up. They are trying, though not very hard, to comfort my mother, who in another era would be considered to be suffering from the vapors. Less tactful in the twenty-first century, I'd say she was losing it. That is, if I didn't know her better, know she was milking it for everything it was worth.

My mother loves attention. As it begins to flag, she swoons and claims to feel faint. Despite four No Smoking signs, my mother insists it's all right for her to light up because, after all, she's in shock. Not to mention that signs, as we know, don't apply to her.

When asked not to smoke, she collapses mournfully in a chair and lets her head loll to the side, all without mussing her hair.

Eventually, the detectives show up to find the

four patrolmen all circled around her, debating whether to administer CPR, smelling salts or simply call the paramedics. I, however, know just what will snap her to attention.

"Detective Scoones," I say loudly. My mother parts the sea of cops.

"We have to stop meeting like this," he says lightly to me, but I can feel him checking me over with his eyes, making sure I'm all right while pretending not to care.

"What have you got in those pants?" my mother asks him, coming to her feet and staring at his crotch accusingly. "*Baydar?* Everywhere we Bayers are, you turn up. You don't expect me to buy that this is a coincidence, I hope."

Drew tells my mother that it's nice to see her, too, and asks if it's his fault that her daughter seems to attract disasters.

Charming to be made to feel like the bearer of a plague.

He asks how I am.

"Just peachy," I tell him. "I seem to be making a habit of finding dead bodies, my mother is driving me crazy and the catering hall I booked two freakin' years ago for Dana's bat mitzvah has just been shut down by the Board of Health!"

"Glad to see your luck's finally changing," he says, giving me a quick squeeze around the shoulders before turning his attention to the patrolmen, asking what they've got, whether they've taken any statements, moved anything, all the sort of stuff you see on TV, without any of the drama. That is, if you don't count my mother's threats to faint every few minutes when she senses no one's paying attention to her.

Mario tells his waitstaff to bring everyone espresso, which I decline because I'm wired enough. Drew pulls him aside and a minute later I'm handed a cup of coffee that smells divinely of Kahlúa.

The man knows me well. Too well.

His partner, whom I've met once or twice, says he'll interview the kitchen staff. Drew asks Mario if he minds if he takes statements from the patrons first and gets to him and the waitstaff afterward.

"No, no," Mario tells him. "Do the patrons first." Drew raises his eyebrow at me like he wants to know if I get the double entendre. I try to look bored.

"What is it with you and murder victims?" he asks me when we sit down at a table in the corner.

I search them out so that I can see you again, I almost say, but I'm afraid it will sound desperate instead of sarcastic.

My mother, lighting up and daring him with a look to tell her not to, reminds him that *she* was the one to find the body.

Drew asks what happened *this time*. My mother tells him how the man in the john was "taken" with me, couldn't take his eyes off me and blatantly flirted with both of us. To his credit, Drew doesn't laugh, but his smirk is undeniable to the trained eye. And I've had my eye trained on him for nearly a year now.

"While he was noticing you," he asks me, "did *you* notice anything about him? Was he waiting for anyone? Watching for anything?"

I tell him that he didn't appear to be waiting or watching. That he made no phone calls, was fairly intent on eating and did, indeed, flirt with my mother. This last bit Drew takes with a grain of salt, which was the way it was intended.

"And he had a short conversation with Mario," I tell him. "I think he might have been unhappy with the food, though he didn't send it back."

Drew asks what makes me think he was dissatisfied, and I tell him that the discussion seemed acrimonious and that Mario looked distressed when he left the table. Drew makes a note and says he'll look into it and asks about anyone else in the restaurant. Did I see anyone who didn't seem to belong, anyone who was watching the victim, anyone looking suspicious?

"Besides my mother?" I ask him, and Mom huffs and blows her cigarette smoke in my direction.

I tell him that there were several deliveries, the kitchen staff going in and out the back door to grab a smoke. He stops me and asks what I was doing checking out the back door of the restaurant.

Proudly—because, while he was off forgetting me, dropping by only once in a while to say hi to Jesse, my son, or drop something by for one of my daughters that he thought they might like, I was getting on with my life—I tell him that I'm decorating the place.

He looks genuinely impressed. "Commercial customers? That's great," he says. Okay, that's what he *ought* to say. What he actually says is "Whatever pays the bills."

"Howard Rosen, the famous restaurant critic, got her the job," my mother says. "You met him—the good-looking, distinguished gentleman with the *real* job, something to be proud of. I guess you've never read his reviews in *Newsday*."

Drew, without missing a beat, tells her that Howard's reviews are on the top of his list, as soon as he learns how to read.

"I only meant—" my mother starts, but both of us assure her that we know just what she meant.

"So," Drew says. "Deliveries?"

I tell him that Mario would know better than I, but that I saw vegetables come in, maybe fish and linens.

"This is the second restaurant job Howard's got her," my mother tells Drew.

"At least she's getting *something* out of the relationship," he says.

"If he were here," my mother says, ignoring the insinuation, "he'd be comforting her instead of interrogating her. He'd be making sure we're both all right after such an ordeal."

"I'm sure he would," Drew agrees, then looks me in the eyes as if he's measuring my tolerance for shock. Quietly he adds, "But then maybe he doesn't know just what strong stuff your daughter's made of."

It's the closest thing to a tender moment I can expect from Drew Scoones. My mother breaks the spell. "She gets that from me," she says.

Both Drew and I take a minute, probably to pray that's all I inherited from her.

"I'm just trying to save you some time and effort," my mother tells him. "My money's on Howard."

Drew withers her with a look and mutters something that sounds suspiciously like "fool's gold." Then he excuses himself to go back to work.

I catch his sleeve and ask if it's all right for us to leave. He says sure, he knows where we live. I say goodbye to Mario. I assure him that I will have some sketches for him in a few days, all the while hoping that this murder doesn't cancel his redecorating plans. I need the money desperately, the alternative being borrowing from my parents and being strangled by the strings.

My mother is strangely quiet all the way to her house. She doesn't tell me what a loser Drew Scoones is—despite his good looks—and how I was obviously drooling over him. She doesn't ask me where Howard is taking me tonight or warn me not to tell my father about what happened because he will worry about us both and no doubt insist we see our respective psychiatrists.

She fidgets nervously, opening and closing her purse over and over again.

"You okay?" I ask her. After all, she's just found a dead man on the toilet, and tough as she is that's got to be upsetting.

When she doesn't answer me I pull over to the side of the road.

"Mom?" She refuses to meet my eyes. "You want me to take you to see Dr. Cohen?"

She looks out the window as if she's just realized we're on Broadway in Woodmere. "Aren't we near Marvin's Jewelers?" she asks, pulling something out of her purse.

"What have you got, Mother?" I ask, prying open her fingers to find the murdered man's ring.

"It was on the sink," she says in answer to my dropped jaw. "I was going to get his name and address and have you return it to him so that he could ask you out. I thought it was a sign that the two of you were meant to be together."

"He's dead, Mom. You understand that, right?" I ask. You never can tell when my mother is fine and when she's in la-la land.

"Well, I didn't know that," she shouts at me. "Not at the time."

I ask why she didn't give it to Drew, realize that she wouldn't give Drew the time in a clock shop and add, "…or one of the other policemen?"

"For heaven's sake," she tells me. "The man is dead, Teddi, and I took his ring. How would that look?"

Before I can tell her it looks just the way it is, she pulls out a cigarette and threatens to light it.

"I mean, really," she says, shaking her head like it's my brains that are loose. "What does he need with it now?"

Silhouette®

SPECIAL EDITION™

Logan's Legacy Revisited

**THE LOGAN FAMILY IS BACK
WITH SIX NEW STORIES.**

Beginning in January 2007 with

THE COUPLE
MOST LIKELY TO

by

LILIAN DARCY

Tragedy drove them apart. Reunited eighteen
years later, their attraction was once again
undeniable. But had time away changed
Jake Logan enough to let him face his fears
and commit to the woman he once loved?

Silhouette

n o c t u r n e™

WAS HE HER SAVIOR
OR HER NIGHTMARE?

HAUNTED
LISA CHILDS

Years ago, Ariel and her sisters were separated for
their own protection. Now the man who vowed
revenge on her family has resumed the hunt, and
Ariel must warn her sisters before it's too late.
The closer she comes to finding them, the more
secretive her fiancé becomes. Can she trust the man
she plans to spend eternity with? Or has he been
waiting for the perfect moment to destroy her?

On sale December 2006.

In February, expect *MORE*
from

HARLEQUIN®
Romance.

as it increases to six titles per month.

What's to come...

Rancher and Protector

Part of the
Western Weddings
miniseries

BY JUDY CHRISTENBERRY

The Boss's
Pregnancy Proposal

BY RAYE MORGAN

Don't miss February's
incredible line up of authors!

REQUEST YOUR FREE BOOKS!
2 FREE NOVELS PLUS 2 FREE GIFTS!

SPECIAL EDITION™

Life, Love and Family!

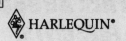

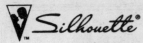

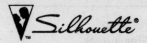

COMING NEXT MONTH